"Lexi, we need to go. Quickly."

"I
No

"T

Le
gr
th

"W

Iss
ma

Le
he

Iss   p
in

"H

"S

"I

Th
Cc   s
he

"V

She nodded, but wasn't convinced anymore that there was a way out.

Lisa Harris is a Christy Award winner and winner of the Best Inspirational Suspense Novel for 2011 from *RT Book Reviews*. She and her family are missionaries in southern Africa. When she's not working she loves hanging out with her family, cooking different ethnic dishes, photography and heading into the African bush on safari. For more information about her books and life in Africa, visit her website at lisaharriswrites.com.

Books by Lisa Harris

Love Inspired Suspense

Final Deposit
Stolen Identity
Deadly Safari
Taken
Desperate Escape
Desert Secrets

DESERT SECRETS

LISA HARRIS

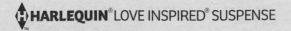 HARLEQUIN® LOVE INSPIRED® SUSPENSE

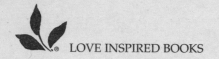 LOVE INSPIRED BOOKS

ISBN-13: 978-0-373-45688-8

Desert Secrets

Copyright © 2017 by Lisa Harris

www.Harlequin.com

Printed in U.S.A.

Because You are my help, I sing in the shadow of Your wings. I cling to You; Your right hand upholds me.
—Psalms 63:7-8

To those who are seeking.
May you find Him when you seek with all your heart.

ONE

Lexi Shannon winced at the sharp sting of her captor's hand across the side of her face. She blinked back the tears, then reached up to wipe away the metallic taste of blood that had pooled in the corner of her mouth.

"I'm going to ask you one last time," the man repeated. "Where is your brother?"

She looked up at his weathered face and forced herself to catch his gaze. "I don't know."

He stood over her in his khaki fatigues, anger flashing in his eyes at her response. "Then we have a problem, because my boss isn't going to like your answer. We know he was in Timbuktu with you."

She pressed her nails into the palms of her hands, determined not to cry. "He was with me, but like I've already told you, he left yesterday morning, and I have no idea where he is now."

He squatted down in front of her, his dark eyes boring through her. "Then tell me again. Everything you know about your brother's visit."

Lexi glanced across the makeshift compound where they'd kept her the last few hours. Past the rustic tents made of animal skins toward the endless ripples of the orange Sahara shimmering in the late afternoon sunlight. There was nothing but the sand in every direction and the raging sun above them.

"Five days ago, Trent came to visit me in Timbuktu," she said, repeating what she'd already told them. "He told me he'd decided he wanted to see some of the world and I was his first stop. He never mentioned you, or your boss, or owing money to anyone. Never mentioned he was in any kind of trouble."

"And the last time you saw him?" he asked.

A small lizard burrowed through the sand in front of her. Lexi drew in a lungful of air, wishing she could disappear as easily as it could.

"When I woke up yesterday morning he was gone," she said. "He left me a note. Said he was sorry, but he'd received an urgent email from someone in the middle of the night—some work-related emergency—and needed to take an early flight out of the country. He said he hadn't wanted to wake me."

"And you didn't find that…odd?"

"Not for Trent."

Which was true. She'd never completely believed most of Trent's stories. Her stepbrother had always been a challenge, tending to hang out with the wrong crowd and make bad decisions. But in spite of his shortcomings, he was still family, and no matter what he'd done now, she didn't want anything terrible to happen to him.

"Amar?" Another man called from the entrance of one of the tents where he stood holding an automatic weapon.

Amar nodded at the other man before turning back to Lexi. "Just know we're not done yet."

He left her sitting in the partial shade, grateful to be alone again. From the moment they'd grabbed her from the site where she'd been overseeing the installation of a water well, she'd tried to pay close attention to her surroundings, looking for any means to get out of this situation. But as far as she could tell, there was no escape from this place. Beyond the four armed guards—and one other prisoner she'd only seen from a distance—all she could see was the unending desert sands surrounding them.

A wave of fatigue washed over Lexi as the reality of her situation began to sink in. She closed her eyes and took in a deep breath, trying to slow her rapid heart rate, and trying to figure out her odds of getting out of here alive. Amar had threatened her repeatedly, trying to force her to tell him what he wanted to know, but how was she supposed to give him information she didn't have?

I'm out of options here, God.

"Thirsty?"

Lexi opened her eyes and looked up, surprised when she saw the other prisoner standing in front of her, holding out a water bottle. "It tastes pretty bad, but at least it's wet."

She studied him for a brief moment. Faded Atlanta Braves T-shirt, cargo shorts and a ball cap shading his bearded face from the sun. She glanced back at her captives, but no one seemed to notice or care that they were talking. And why would they? It wasn't as if they were going anywhere.

"Thanks," Lexi said, taking the plastic water bottle. She took a long drink. He was right. The water was lukewarm and bitter, but she didn't care. "You're an American?"

"I've lived in the States for twenty years, but still hold a German passport. I'm Bret Fischer."

"Lexi Shannon," she said, taking another sip. "How long have you been here?"

"Fifty-seven days."

Her jaw clenched. From where she sat, fifty-seven days seemed like an eternity.

I'm not sure if I can do this, God. Day after day of not knowing if the next moment will be my last...

"My wife didn't want me to come. Kept reminding me that the instability in the region has made kidnapping and hostage taking more frequent." He let out a low chuckle. "I guess she was right."

"Does the terror ever diminish?"

"I wish I could say yes, but so far...no."

"So what keeps you going?" she asked, handing back the water bottle.

He took the bottle, then sat down beside her. "My faith. And knowing my family will keep trying to get me out of here until they find a way."

Her attention shifted momentarily to the nearby tent. Two of the men were arguing about something, making her wish she could understand their language. And making her want to believe that her faith and hope was all she would need to get her through this.

But what if she wasn't strong enough for whatever lay ahead?

"I heard Amar interrogating you," he said, breaking into her thoughts. "Why do they keep asking you about your brother?"

"They say he owes their boss money. A lot of money,

apparently, and he thinks I know where they might find him. He said they'll kill me if I don't help them."

"You're worth more alive than dead."

"Am I? I've heard that the United States won't pay ransoms, and I certainly can't pay back what my brother owes."

"I understand how you feel. Because I have a German passport, they think the country will pay, but if that's true, no one on either side seems to be in a hurry."

She didn't say anything, because there was nothing really to say. Instead, she wiped the sweat off her forehead with the sleeve of her shirt. She'd never again complain about the heat back in Timbuktu—if she were ever able to return. It had to be at least twenty degrees hotter out here.

"What was your brother doing in Mali?" Bret asked, breaking the silence between them.

"He told me he just wanted to come for a visit, though now I'm not so sure." She leaned forward and wrapped her arms around her knees, hating feeling so vulnerable and defenseless. "What about you? You mentioned your wife."

"Becca and I've been married twenty-one years, and have a seventeen-year-old son, Noah." He twisted the gold ring on his left hand. "I was hoping to return with my son next year, but now..."

"Why here?" she asked, realizing what a welcome distraction the conversation was.

"My brother-in-law's a pilot with West African Mission Aviation. They provide medical care and disaster relief. He's the one who connected me to the group I ended up joining."

"I met one of their pilots once." Lexi fiddled with

the hem of her pale blue T-shirt while watching the tent flap flutter in the hot breeze. "His name was Colton."

"Colton... That's my brother-in-law."

"Really?" She looked up and caught Bret's gaze. "Wow. It's a small world, isn't it? Think he's working on a plan to rescue you?"

Bret let out a low laugh. "I'll be honest—the thought has crossed my mind more than once. It wouldn't be easy, but Colton's former military and was involved in another rescue a few months back off the coast of Guinea-Bissau. If anyone could pull it off, he could."

She wanted to believe a rescue was possible. From the brief conversation she'd had with Colton at a local restaurant in Timbuktu a couple months ago, she'd been impressed with the handsome pilot. She'd learned that he did most of his flying for missionaries and aid organizations farther to the west.

"What about you?" Bret asked, taking a sip of the water. "What brought you to Mali?"

"I've been working on sustainable water sources the past nine months. As you probably know, both distribution networks and access to water are a huge concern."

Most nights she was asleep not long after the sun sank below the horizon, exhausted from a long day of dealing with red tape and language barriers. She was over five thousand miles away from her hometown in Southern California—and even further, culturally—but she loved the feeling of accomplishment her work brought. And the feeling that she was doing her part to make the world a better place.

"Lexi..." Bret placed his hand on her shoulder. Amar was walking back toward where they were sitting in the sand, his automatic slung over his shoulder, and a deep frown across his face. "We will find a way out of this. Alive. I promise."

A wave of nausea washed over her. She wanted him to be right, but she also knew that wasn't a promise he could keep.

Colton Landry felt the muscles in his shoulders tense as he went through his prelanding checklist and began his descent toward the isolated airstrip. He glanced out the window of the six-passenger Cessna at the endless terrain below, needing to calm his nerves.

From the first time he'd flown as a sixteen-year-old, he'd discovered there was nothing more exhilarating than catching a bird's-eye view of the earth's surface in a small plane. But today as he flew above the legendary Sahara Desert of North Africa, the view did little to take away the stress knotted in his stomach.

Had it already been almost two months since his brother-in-law had vanished? The phone call to his sister had left them both reeling.

If you don't come up with two million dollars in cash, we will kill him.

He'd read the news articles of the booming business. Kidnapping hostages had proven to be easy money and common across North Africa. And the captors seemingly had both the patience and time to get what they wanted. He knew if he ever planned to see his brother-in-law alive again, he was going to have to take matters into his own hands.

Which was why, when a representative from the Malian army had come to him with a plan, he'd jumped at the chance to make it happen.

They told him they were dealing with a small rogue

band of work-for-hire bearded fighters. All Colton had
to do was fly in with his two suitcases filled with counterfeit money. Once the exchange was made, they'd provide the needed firepower and get the credit for taking
down the group of insurgents that had been plaguing
their northern border.

It was a win-win situation for everyone.

It was also a risk. But the military had taught him
all about taking dangerous chances. And this was one
chance he was willing to take. He'd heard his sister's
frantic voice on the phone and seen the video of Bret
along with the militants' well-rehearsed demands. It
might not be his brother-in-law's best way out, but at
the moment, it was their only option.

Minutes later, Colton landed on the airstrip, a hundred miles from the nearest town. The promised Jeep
was waiting for him next to the landing strip along with
the driver, who introduced himself as Joseph.

"You're late," the other man said, grabbing one of
the suitcases Colton had brought with him off the plane.

"How far to the exchange?" he asked, ignoring the
other man's comment.

"Fifteen minutes tops."

He threw his suitcase into the back of the 4x4, sent
up another prayer for protection for his brother-in-law,
then slipped into the front passenger seat.

Joseph started the engine and headed north along
the sand-covered rolling plains with a few rugged hills
in the distance. "So you are from the United States."

"Yeah."

"I have a brother in Chicago. He moved there over
a decade ago. I always planned to visit, but for some
reason never made it."

The man's English was decent, but Colton wasn't in the mood for chitchat. All he wanted was to get to the meeting place, make the exchange and get his brother-in-law out of here.

"Is our backup ready?" Colton asked.

"Don't worry. They will be there."

"It's kind of hard not to worry." He gripped the armrest as the Jeep flew over a ridge of sand. "My brother-in-law's life is on the line."

"You're clear on the plan?" Joseph asked.

"Once we get to the rendezvous spot, I'll hand them the suitcases, take my brother-in-law and then let the army clean up the mess while we hightail it back to the plane."

He spoke like this was a routine part of his job; one he'd done a dozen times before. But just because he followed the rules didn't mean the kidnappers were planning to follow them, as well. He wasn't naive enough to ignore the possibility that this could end very, very badly.

Because this entire situation was far from routine. He'd spent hundreds of hours shuttling people to remote places like where they were right now. Allowing people to do water and medical projects and other types of development. A plane was the most effective means of reaching an out-of-the-way village when the alternative was driving hundreds of miles over rough terrain. But this—the outcome of this mission—was completely out of his control.

"You sound like you've done this before," Joseph said.

"Hardly. But I don't have a choice. They're going to kill my brother-in-law if I don't do something."

There were also political ramifications to consider. He knew terrorist groups took in millions of dollars from kidnappings. Money was funneled through proxy networks, often disguised as foreign aid. He didn't like playing a part in that scheme. But what else was he supposed to do?

Twenty-five minutes later, Colton saw a cluster of tent flaps blowing beneath the next ridge. If all went according to plan, in another five minutes he'd be making his way back to the plane with Bret. Then he and his brother would be flying toward Morocco and freedom.

I need this plan to work, God...

Because Bret's life depended on it.

Joseph stopped the vehicle a dozen yards from the nearest tent. "I'll wait here for you."

Colton nodded, then stepped out of the Jeep and grabbed the suitcases, hesitating briefly before heading toward the camp. This had to be the right place, but there were no signs of Bret or his captors. No movement in the distance except the hot wind that never stopped blowing.

He glanced at the ridge. If the Malian army wasn't here, right now, they were all going to end up dead.

A man with a thick beard stepped out of the shadows of one of the tents and into the sunlight. "You have what we asked for?"

"I've got the suitcases." Colton walked slowly forward with one in each hand, his heart pounding with each step against the shifting sand.

"Set them down on the ground in front of you."

Colton gripped the handles of the suitcases. "I want to see my brother-in-law."

"That's not how it's going to work." The man raised

his automatic weapon. "First, I see the money. Then we'll talk about your brother."

Colton glanced up at the ridge. There was still no movement. And he didn't have a plan B.

He hesitated, then set down the suitcases and took a step back. "Where's my brother-in-law?"

"Don't worry. He's here."

Bret appeared at the entrance of one of the tents gripping a backpack in his hand.

Colton resisted the urge to run to him and pull him into a bear hug, but there was no time for a family reunion. "We need to get you out of here—"

"Wait," Bret said. "There's another prisoner."

A young woman ducked out of the tent behind Bret, the wind tugging on the ends of her dark, shoulder-length hair. His mind fought to place the familiar face. He'd met her before. They'd chatted briefly...

Lexi.

The man shouted at her to get back. "She's not going with you."

Another man grabbed her arm. She screamed, trying to fight back. A second later, a bullet slammed into the man, dropping him to the ground beside her. She stood frozen. Blood spatter dotted her khaki pants. Colton reacted instantly, ignoring the men shouting around them as he ran to her, then pulled her toward the only cover there was behind one of the tents.

"Are you hurt?" he asked.

"I don't think so."

He looked back up at the ridge. Half a dozen men in military uniforms appeared along the ridge at the edge of the camp. He let out a sharp sigh of relief. The army had arrived. Now it was up to him to get them safely out of here.

"Follow me. We need to go now." He grabbed Lexi's hand and started running back toward the Jeep with Bret right behind them, praying the army would be able to hold the kidnappers off. "I've got a driver waiting for us."

He shoved back the worst-case scenarios flooding through his mind as he caught sight of the approaching vehicle. They'd almost made it through the most difficult part, getting away from their captors in one piece. Now all he had to do was ensure they got to the airstrip, got the plane in the air and flew them out of this nightmare.

TWO

While Lexi's mind fought to hold on to reality, Colton held her hand and they ran across the sand and away from the sounds of gunfire. She'd been kidnapped by rebels, taken to an unknown location in the middle of the desert, only to be rescued by a man she'd dreamed about. It sounded more like a movie than her own fairly routine life.

She tripped on a bulge in the sand, but Colton caught her, ensuring she kept her balance. She glanced down at her bloodstained pants, before she started running again. Unlike her nighttime imaginings of Colton, this was no dream. A man had been murdered next to her. She was running for her life in the middle of the Sahara, praying that one of those bullets she heard behind her didn't hit her or one of the men escaping with her.

Bret had mentioned how he'd hoped his brother-in-law had a plan to rescue them, but at the time that had seemed impossible. And with men who had nothing to lose, she could have easily been kept for months, even years. She knew what happened to people like her who were snatched up and disappeared. It was a place she hadn't wanted to imagine for herself.

"This is my driver, Joseph," Colton said, as they neared the Jeep. "He'll get us out of here in one piece."

Colton helped her into backseat of the vehicle next to Bret, then scrambled into the front passenger seat. The second his door closed, Joseph pushed on the accelerator and headed back across the sand in the direction they'd come from.

Lexi pulled the seat belt across her lap and buckled it, working to slow her breathing both from exertion and pure terror.

"Are you both okay?" Colton asked.

"We will be once we put enough miles between us and those men. This is Lexi Shannon, by the way," Bret said, making a quick introduction. "And I'm sure she'd agree that your timing couldn't have been more perfect."

"We met once in Timbuktu," Colton said, looking at her with those unforgettable smoky gray eyes.

"You remember?" Her hands gripped the armrest as Joseph sped across the bumpy terrain that even with a seat belt on made her feel as if she were about to fly through the window.

"I do. Are you sure you're okay?" he asked her.

"I think so." She tried not to think about the blood-stained pants.

"How long have you been here?" Colton asked.

"They grabbed me yesterday morning outside Timbuktu." She tried to suppress the wave of emotion that came with the memories. "Then brought me to the camp early this morning."

A day earlier and he would have missed her. A day later—she hated to think what they might have done to her given more time.

Bret reached up and squeezed Colton's shoulder. "You can't imagine how good it is to see you. The two of us discussed your taking part in a rescue, but I honestly didn't think it was possible. Where in the world did you come up with two million dollars?"

Colton turned back around, as the camp faded into the distance along with the sounds of gunfire. "I didn't."

"Didn't what?" Bret asked.

"I didn't have the money. Not real bills, anyway. It was counterfeit."

Bret leaned forward. "Counterfeit?"

The surprise in Bret's voice mirrored her own. Arriving without the ransom was a risk that could have easily cost not just her and Bret's life, but Colton's, as well. And yet the plan had worked. He had somehow managed to grab both Bret and her while the rebels had taken the fall with the army's bullets.

"I decided to show up with the Malian army instead," Colton said. "I know it sounds crazy, but when Becca and I couldn't come up with the two million, it was the only real option we had."

"You're kidding me." Bret shook his head. "If they'd opened those suitcases and discovered what was inside, or if those soldiers hadn't shown up…"

"But none of that happened," Colton said. "And now the army's going to play cleanup *and* you're safe."

A shadow crossed Bret's face. "How is Becca?"

"My sister's a strong woman, but it's been a tough few weeks for both her and Noah. The waiting and not knowing…"

"They're what kept me going."

"We'll call her as soon as we can, I promise. Let's

just focus on getting out of here first and making sure we're all safe."

Lexi glanced out the window at the miles and miles of endless sand. Dunes loomed to the west then spread out flat in front of them and to the east. She was still breathing hard. Her heart still pounding. She wasn't going to feel safe for a very long time.

Movement out of the corner of her eye caught her attention from behind them.

She turned to look out the back window as the Jeep bounced across the uneven ground. A vehicle followed.

"Colton…" She could hear the panic in her voice as she spoke.

"What's wrong?"

She stared out the back of the Jeep. "There's someone behind us, and they're closing in."

"I thought the army was supposed to clean up while we made a getaway," Joseph said, pushing on the accelerator.

Lexi gripped her fingers tighter around the armrest. When she was a teenager and they'd lived in California, her stepfather had raced dirt bikes up the local sand dunes. He taken her out a few times and taught her about safety. Which was why she knew that this wasn't the place to be running for their lives. She'd seen firsthand how easy it was to flip a vehicle. Or the potential of getting stuck in the sand. Add to that, if the tire pressure was too high, the handling ability of the 4x4 would be affected.

There were so many things that could go wrong.

"What do we do now?" Bret asked.

"We need to figure out plan B," Colton said.

"Which is?" Joseph asked.

"Drive straight up the dune," Colton said.

"I was just thinking the same thing," Joseph said.

"You've got to be kidding! That's crazy!" Lexi grabbed the headrest and leaned forward. "It's too easy to roll."

"I'm pretty sure that other vehicle doesn't have enough power to make it over the top," Joseph said, apparently buying into the idea.

"And if we don't make it all the way up?" Lexi asked.

"We'll end up rolling back down the dune," Joseph said. "But that won't happen."

Lexi frowned. "And this vehicle...you think it can handle it?"

"I'm not sure we have a choice. Which means everyone needs to grab on to something now."

Lexi leaned back in her seat and felt the pull of gravity fighting against the vehicle as Joseph took a sharp left and headed up the dune. What if they didn't make it to the top? And even if they did go over the hill unscathed and lost whoever was behind them, they still weren't out of the woods yet. There could be other insurgents coming after them, and then there was Colton's brother-in-law. He was weak after two months of captivity and needed to be checked out by a doctor.

Joseph had his foot on the accelerator, fighting with the engine to keep up the momentum. If he tried to turn or cross the slope, they'd end up popping a tire or flipping the car. And if they didn't maintain their speed they'd never make it.

Lexi turned around just in time to see the other vehicle rolling back down the steep hill. There was still a chance they would meet the same end as they weren't at the top yet.

Finally they crested the top of the ridge. Joseph had been right.

"I think your zany plan worked," Bret said.

Lexi let out a lungful of pent-up air, and realized she'd been holding her breath.

"We're not out of here yet, but we're close," Joseph said, reading her thoughts. "Your Cessna's parked about ten minutes ahead."

Lexi caught the worry in Colton's expression as Joseph sped across the desert. All they had to do now was make it to Colton's plane and take off before anyone else tried to stop them.

Get them in the air and fly them out of here.

A piece of cake, Colton thought, still trying to convince himself they were out of danger as the Cessna took off from the runway fifteen minutes later. Thanks to Joseph's skilled driving, they'd made it to the plane.

There was no human settlement for as far as he could see. Nothing growing in the harsh desert sands except for a few scraggly bushes. Nothing to stop them. They might actually make it out of here in one piece after all.

Colton felt the muscles in his shoulders begin to relax as the six-passenger aircraft continued climbing toward its cruising altitude. He drew in a deep breath, then glanced down at the familiar terrain below him from the pilot's seat. Endless ripples of orange shimmered in the afternoon sunlight.

He glanced behind him at the seat where his brother-in-law had his head back and his eyes closed. Colton took a moment to study Bret's profile. His beard had grown, his face was tanned and he'd lost a significant amount of weight. But he was alive. And for now, that was all that mattered.

Besides the loss of weight, he still looked fairly strong, though there was no way at this point to measure the emotional effects of what he'd gone through. Now he just needed to get Bret home.

Colton shifted his attention to the passenger sitting beside him, letting his gaze linger longer than necessary before turning back to the controls. Lexi Shannon had intrigued him during the one, brief time he'd met her. First impressions had revealed she was smart, compassionate, adventurous and, on top of that, beautiful. Not that he was interested in pursuing anything at this point. A broken relationship was one of the factors that had sealed the deal on him taking a job flying missionary bush planes across North Africa. There was no way he was ready to hand in his pilot's license for another rocky romance.

"You okay?" he asked her through his headset, deciding that a bit of conversation couldn't hurt. He needed a distraction, and he was pretty sure she did, as well.

She turned and smiled at him with a mixture of both determination and fatigue in her gaze. "Besides the fact that my adrenaline's still pumping, and I will probably forever be leery of men in fatigues...yeah. Or I will be...eventually."

Colton laughed. "I don't blame you."

Her dark eyes intensified. "Thank you. You risked a lot to get us out of there."

"All in a day's work."

"Something tells me that today was anything but normal," she said. "At least I hope so."

"I don't know. Rescuing a damsel in distress isn't a bad way to spend my time if you ask me. And on top of that you can't beat the view from up here," he said. And besides, after today's flight, the chances of him seeing her again were pretty slim.

"Absolutely stunning." She shot him a smile that somehow managed to melt away one of the outer layers of protection he'd built up around his heart.

"See that row of camels?" Colton ignored his heart and pointed toward a thin line of camels that looked like a trail of smoke against the sand.

Lexi leaned forward, searched the landscape below them, then nodded. "Wow. One of the things I want to do before I move back to the US is camel trekking along with a night spent in the desert. I've heard that both the night sky and the sunrises are incredible."

"They are," Colton said. "Though here's an interesting fact. Did you know that camels really don't store water the way most people think? Their humps are actually made of fat, allowing them to keep their body temperature down."

Lexi laughed. "I didn't know I was getting a rescuer, a pilot *and* a tour guide today."

"Camels also have three eyelids," he added with a grin. "Though don't get too excited. That's pretty much the extent of my knowledge."

Lexi laughed again. "When I first flew here, I arrived at night, then we drove in the rest of the way, so this is my first up-close view of the desert from the air. But I know you make these flights all the time. Does it ever become routine? At least when you're not rescuing damsels in distress?"

"Routine?" He shook his head. "Hardly. This is the third largest desert in the world after the Arctic and Antarctica. Some might call it barren—and a lot of it is—but I find it fascinating. Have you ever been up in a Cessna before?"

"My grandfather's a pilot, though he doesn't fly as much as he used to. I always wanted to take flying lessons myself, but for some reason I've never taken the time to learn."

"It's never too late." Colton said. "What does your grandfather fly?"

"He used to have a 1979 Super Viking."

Colton let out a low whistle. "I flew one of those once. Loved it."

"He named her Abigail after my grandmother. She—well, both the plane and my grandmother were his pride and joy."

"I can imagine. At least for the plane, that is." Colton chuckled. "Single-engine, four seat, high performance. The one I flew handled like a dream."

"I have a feeling you and my grandfather would hit it off. He's a veteran with dozen's of stories to tell. I keep telling him he needs to write them all down."

"I'd love to hear them sometime—"

The sound of an explosion drowned out their conversation. The entire plane shook and started veering toward the right.

Lexi pressed her hand against the window to hold herself upright. "What in the world just happened?"

He glanced out the window, his own heart hammering as the plane started to dive.

You've got to be kidding...

"Colton?" Bret grabbed his shoulder from behind.

"Looks like we've been hit," Colton said.

"What?" He caught the panic in Lexi's voice as she spoke. "You can't be serious?"

"Trust me, I wish I wasn't," Colton said, managing to pull them out of the dive.

At least for the moment.

"Hit with what?" Bret asked.

"I don't know, but whoever followed us must have brought some firepower with him."

"How serious is it?"

"Let's just say, I'm going to try to keep this bird in the air as long as I can, but eventually I'm going to have to find a place to land. And probably sooner rather than later."

He picked up the radio to contact his base back in Timbuktu, but all he could hear was static. Whatever hit them must have knocked out the antenna. Glancing out the window again, he saw smoke coming out the side of the plane.

"What do you see down there?" he asked.

"I think there's a vehicle. Maybe the one that was following us. I don't know," Lexi said.

"Whoever's down there has to have some kind of surface-to-air missile," Colton fought to keep the plane in the air. He needed to get them as far away as he could from the men on the ground before he brought the aircraft down.

He let out a sharp huff of air. Actually landing the plane could turn out to be least of their worries. If they managed to survive the landing and avoid whoever was after them, they were still going to have to deal with the harsh elements of the terrain below. With its shifting sand dunes, barren plateaus, and limited water and vegetation, most people couldn't even fathom the actual size and dangers of the desert that engulfed northern Africa. He scanned the horizon. All he could see was the miles and miles of sand that spread out around them. The nearest town was hours away by foot—if they could even find it—and when night fell the soaring temperatures were going to drop.

Colton tried to shove back the worst-case scenarios flooding through his mind in order to deal with the emergency at hand. "I need you both to tighten your seat belts. This is going to get rough."

Thirty minutes later, the engine sputtered and died. He reacted automatically thanks to hours of practicing emergency scenarios and began planning his approach. Because no matter what happened in the next few seconds, he had to be in control of the aircraft. Full flaps, gears down, wings level...

God, I could really use your help right now.

Colton held his breath, straining to keep his plane just above the stall speed as he dropped in altitude and made his approach. The theory of landing an aircraft on a soft surface was fairly simple. Control the airspeed of the plane so the wings could support the weight of the craft as long as possible, then touch down at a minimum speed with the nose at a high pitch as the wheels made contact with the ground.

Whether or not their actual landing ended up to be that straightforward with a section of the plane hit was going to be a whole other story.

THREE

The impact jolted Colton forward as he touched down the plane, then managed to slide to a stop. Silence engulfed the cabin. His lungs let out a swish of air, but he wasn't done yet. He needed to get the three of them off the aircraft.

"Are you two okay?" He glanced at Lexi as he undid his seat belt before moving to open the door. Her face had paled, but she nodded. Bret was also clearly shaken, but seemed okay, as well.

He waited for them to disembark, still needing to determine the damage to the aircraft. Frustration simmered to the surface as he made his initial assessment. Inside the cockpit, the radio was dead, which likely meant the instrument panel had been damaged on impact, and they'd lost their only way to communicate. Outside the plane, the damage was just as extensive. Beyond the hole left by the attack, one landing gear plus the nose of the plane had been sheared off. There was no way they were flying out of here.

He joined the others beneath the shadow of the wing, his forehead already beaded with sweat from the heat. He shrugged off his jacket.

"What can I do to help?" Lexi asked.

Colton glanced up at sun that had already begun its descent and ran through his options. There was still a strong chance that his team would be able to find them via the plane's GPS tracker. But for the moment they were on their own. And from his military experience, he knew firsthand how quickly a situation like this could spiral out of control. If they were going to survive, it was going to take them working together and not panicking.

"It's going to be dark before long," he said, quickly taking charge, "which means we need to be prepared to stay here tonight."

"What about going for help?" Bret asked. "There's got to be a village nearby. Because if whoever shot us down finds us…"

"That's an option, but we have no idea how far the nearest village is, and with the sun setting, we don't have time to find it. At least here with the plane's emergency rations, we've got shelter, food and enough water for the time being. And it's better than heading out unprepared and getting lost. When my team discovers we didn't make it to Morocco, they'll start looking for this plane. And if they can track us via the GPS—"

"*If* they can track the GPS?" Lexi tugged at the bottom of her T-shirt.

Colton shook his head. "With no way to communicate with them, I can't be a hundred percent sure they're getting the signal. But if they are—and I'm assuming they are—we should be in Morocco by tomorrow."

But if his team wasn't able to receive the signal and track the plane, he knew that surviving the landing intact had been only one of many hurdles they were liable to face. Because statistically, the odds were against them. The average healthy person exposed fully to the sun in this environment wouldn't last a day without water, and then there were other dangers, as well—like snakes, scorpions and dust storms that were as unpredictable as they were deadly.

"What do you need me to do?" Bret asked. "I could take a look at the radio. It can't be much different from one of Noah's science projects I've helped him with over the years."

"Are you up to it?" Colton asked.

"If it's a way to get help, I'm up for anything."

"Just remember, both of you, that with the temperatures as high as they are, we need to conserve both our energy and our water, and stay out of the direct sun as much as possible. Covering your heads and the back of your necks will help, as well."

"What about me?" Lexi asked.

"I'll need help sorting through the emergency rations."

"Of course."

"But first…" He walked to the hold on the side of the plane where the emergency rations were stored, thankful nothing looked damaged, and pulled out a small suitcase from the side of the plane. "I brought a couple changes of clothes for Bret, figuring he'd probably lost some weight. And while they might not fit perfectly…"

He handed her the chocolate-brown cargo pants and a black V-neck T-shirt.

Lexi looked down at her own bloodstained pants. "Anything is better than what I'm wearing now. Thank you."

Colton nodded, then undid the top button of his shirt, while she walked around to the other side of the plane to change. But he couldn't shake the uneasiness that had settled over him. Because he hadn't told either of them the entire truth. Their emergency landing had taken them way off course, which meant even with his maps, finding the nearest village in this barren terrain wasn't going to be easy. And on top of that, every hour they were stuck here was another hour for the insurgents to find them.

Lexi finished changing into the cargo pants Colton had just given her, pulling the drawstring as tight as she could. They were too long and even cinched tightly they were still too big, but she didn't care. She was just glad she didn't have to wear the bloodstained clothes any longer. And grateful to be alive—though the thought of being stranded in the middle of the Sahara terrified her almost as much as being kidnapped had.

She shoved away thoughts of dehydration, heat stroke and scorpions as she came back around to where Colton was already working.

"Cute outfit," he said, looking up from the pile of supplies he'd pulled out of the plane.

"Funny," she said, returning his grin. "How long will these supplies last?"

"Several days, but my mission will find us before then," he said, grabbing the last jug of water.

"At least you're prepared," she said, hoping she sounded more confident than she felt.

"Our entire fleet carries survival kits appropriate to the region," he said. "First aid, food rations, water, blankets… "

"Sounds as if you've been through this before."

"Two tours in Afghanistan taught me a thing or two about survival."

"I'd like to hear some of your stories."

If they got out of here.

She pushed aside the negative thought. Of course they'd find a way out. They had to.

"How cold does it get out here at night?" she asked.

"It's possible to drop below zero after the sun sets, though thankfully it's not that bad this time of year. It's the heat we have to worry about right now. Dehydration can set in quickly."

He pulled out a narrow box filled with packaged ready-to-eat meals—and set them next to the blankets. At least they wouldn't go hungry.

"We need to pull out everything we'll need from now until morning," he told her. "Primarily sleeping bags, food and water."

She worked beside Colton, remembering details from the first time she'd met him. It had been a quick introduction made by mutual friends at a local restaurant. They'd spent a couple minutes chatting before going their separate ways.

She'd dreamed of the sandy-haired pilot that night, but at the time she'd ignored the attraction. She thought she'd ever see him again, and figured that the chances of them running into each other were slim on this vast continent. And besides that, any feelings of attraction she might feel toward him were completely unwanted. Long-distance relationships didn't work. She'd discovered that firsthand after falling for the last guy she dated.

At first she thought the six-foot three hunk she met

through a mutual friend was perfect. Evan was funny and smart and could always make her laugh no matter what her mood. But after they'd been dating for eight months, Evan took a job in London working as an internal communications manager for a US bank, and it quickly became clear that his communication skills—at least when it came to a relationship—were severely limited. In the end all he'd managed to do was break her heart.

That had been at least part of her motivation to take a year away from her job as an environmental engineer and spend it in Mali. It had taken her family a while to embrace her decision. Her stepfather in particular was convinced she'd left for the ends of the earth. And in a way she had. But in her mind that wasn't a bad thing. Living here had given her time to catch her breath, refocus her goals and start to figure out what she wanted out of life. And beyond that grassroots desire to make a difference, it had helped her with another thing she'd been looking for.

Closure over her mother's death.

Today's events, though, had quickly overshadowed any progress she'd made in figuring out her next step in life.

"Lexi."

She felt his hand against her arm and took in a deep breath.

"You sure you're okay."

"Sorry." She blinked back the unwanted tears. "A couple hours ago, I was trying to wrap my mind around the possibility of spending the next few months in some insurgent camp, and now this…"

"Help is on its way. Even if Bret can't get the radio fixed, there's still the GPS tracker."

"So what happens until then?" she asked, forcing herself to push the past back where it belonged. "We spend the night here, then head to the nearest village first thing in the morning?"

Colton hesitated as he pulled out the last Kelvalite blanket.

"Colton…what is it?" She saw the worry in his eyes. There was something he hadn't told her.

He hesitated a moment longer, then caught her gaze. "While what I said is true, I think you need to know that getting out of here might not be that simple."

Lexi was scared. He could see it in her eyes. But at the moment there was nothing he could to do change it. He hadn't seen any villages from the air. The only thing he had seen as they made their rocky landing was mile after mile of endless sand.

"What do you mean getting out of here might not be that simple?" she asked.

He handed her the last blanket, debating how much he should tell her. "Our emergency landing took us off course."

She sucked in a lungful of air, then blew it out slowly. "How far off course?"

"I'm not sure." He turned to face her, catching her gaze. "But if my team isn't able to track us…we're going to be on our own."

"On our own?" she repeated.

"*If* they can't track us."

He took a swig of cold water from his insulated thermos, hoping it would help counteract the fatigue setting in from the unrelenting heat and the headache that had started. At least the temperature would start dropping soon, and they had enough emergency rations for a couple of days. But beyond that, it was going to be a race against the clock to find their way out of here. And the odds, unfortunately, were far from being in their favor.

Bret stepped out of the plane. The determined set of his jaw told Colton he hadn't been successful.

Colton handed him a bottle of water. "Bad news?"

"I can't get any reception at all. Something must have shorted out, and I'm not sure it can be fixed."

Colton's muscles tensed. In the military he'd been dropped into combat zones and faced roadside bombs. But today he didn't have the backing of a special ops team. His passengers were civilians who weren't used to facing hostile situations. And in an environment like this, anything—and everything—could go wrong.

"Okay." Colton worked to keep his voice sounding upbeat. "Worst-case scenario is that we're stuck out here a day or two until my team can pick us up, but we've got enough food and water to last us a few days."

But they all knew that being found by their abductors first was more likely.

"I think I've about worn myself out for now," Bret said. "I just need a short nap in the shade of the plane, and I think I'll be okay in an hour or two."

Colton grabbed a blanket from the pile. "Are you sure all you need is a rest?"

"I'll be fine. Just need to store up some energy."

Colton watched his brother-in-law find himself a spot in the shade on top of the blanket. "I'm worried about him. He's been though quite an ordeal. He needs to be looked over by a doctor."

"He will be," Lexi assured him, then shot him a half smile. "Because you were right. We're going to get out of here and we have enough supplies to last us until then."

Colton stopped and caught her gaze. "Tell me more about your brother."

Lexi blew out a short breath. "I don't know much more than I've already said. The guys who work for the man he owes money to took me, hoping I could lead them to Trent. Except I have no idea where he is."

Colton shoved his hands into his front pockets. "Are the two of you close?"

"Not really. He's my stepbrother," Lexi said. "My father died when I was thirteen. My mother remarried two years later, so Trent and I didn't really grow up together. And he's always been a bit of a…challenge."

"Sounds like it."

"From what I got out of the men in the short time I was there, he's been embezzling money from a business partner. I think it had something to do with gun running."

"Gun running?" Colton frowned. Clearly whatever Trent had gotten himself involved in, he'd messed with the wrong people.

"I guess I shouldn't be surprised," Lexi said. "When he stayed with me, he was out most nights, keeping strange hours. If only I had known…if I had seen or heard something I would have confronted him." There was no inflection in her voice as she stared out across the cloudless sky. "It might end up costing us all our lives."

Colton rubbed the back of his neck, but it did little

to relieve the growing tension. "You're not responsible for his actions."

"You're wrong." Tears welled in her eyes as she looked up at him. "I should have seen what he was doing...noticed that something wasn't right—"

"And then what?" He ran his hand down her arm until his fingers caught her hand. "This wasn't your fault."

He studied her in the shadow of the plane. The cargo pants and T-shirt he'd given her hung a bit loose on her figure, but still managed to look both comfortable and flattering. He had a feeling she was the kind of person who could fit in pretty much anywhere. Whether it was a corporate board meeting in the States wearing business attire, or doing fieldwork in the middle of an African village.

In another place and time, he could see himself taking the initiative to get to know her. But after Maggie, he had no desire to jump into another relationship. Ever. Spending his days flying across North Africa had become the perfect remedy for a broken heart. He loved the freedom it brought. The time spent in the air where he felt the closest to his Creator, where he could do some good, and where the past seemed the furthest away. It certainly wasn't a life he planned to let go of any time soon.

And everything that had happened today had only managed to remind him that life was volatile, and how everything could change in the blink of an eye.

"I'm worried, Colton."

He caught the vulnerability in her eyes as she spoke and felt a crazy urge to draw her into his arms and tell her everything was going to be all right. That he'd make sure they got to the nearest airport and then on home to the States safely. But he couldn't make her any promises. They were still at the mercy of the desert, and the men who'd shot down their plane.

He brushed his hand against her arm. "We're going to figure this out. I promise."

"But in the meantime, there has to be something else we can do," she said.

"The plane's beyond repair. Bret's sleeping. So for now about the only thing we can do is wait. How about sitting down with me to watch the sunset in the meantime?"

Because he needed to spend the next hour thinking about something—anything—other than the mess they were in, and he knew he wasn't the only one.

FOUR

Lexi hesitated at Colton's suggestion, but already, the sky had captured her attention with its spectacular show of pinks, reds and oranges, lighting the sand in its golden hues. Before long the colors would shift to shades of blue until the vast sky faded into darkness.

"Come on," he said. "You can tell me more about what you've been doing here."

He led her a dozen or so feet from the plane toward a spot where they could have a front row seat to the incredible nightly display and sat down beside her. "I know you're working here with a water program. What did you do back in the States?"

She settled into the space beside Colton, mesmerized by the scene in front of her. "I got a degree in engineering, then started working for a company that provides technical support to both public and private clients, specializing in environmental and marine engineering."

"Sounds interesting."

"It was, actually. At some point, though, I started doing a bunch of research on third-world countries and their infrastructure, particularly their access to clean water, and what I found shocked me. Almost a billion people are without access to safe drinking water. Two and a half billion don't have adequate sanitation facilities. And somewhere around three and a half million people die every year because of this."

"Wow. I knew the figures were high, but I had no idea it was that bad."

"I probably sound like I'm reading a textbook, don't I? My dad tells me the reason I came to work in North Africa was because of watching *Casablanca* too many times." Lexi laughed at the memory. "But the truth is that this is a subject I feel passionate about. And this became a place where I could live out my faith and hopefully make a difference in the world. And as small as it might be, I've seen it change lives."

"You're wrong about one thing."

She looked up at him. "What's that?"

"It's no small difference you're making. To the people you impact, it means everything. The fact that their families now have clean water and they don't have all the water-related ailments they used to have. The fact that their kids don't get as sick so they can go to school."

She stared out across the open sand, amazed once more at all the colors in the sky. The vastness of both the sky and the desert reminded her that they weren't alone. That the God who had created all of this was still here and real and knew exactly what was going on. Which was why, despite everything that had happened over the past few days, she was beginning to relax.

"What about you?" she asked. "Why are you here?"

"A lot of the same reasons, I guess. After leaving the military, I decided I was done with the service, but not with flying. Bret introduced me to an organization looking for pilots. At first I was pretty skeptical, but I knew I didn't want to teach flying, wasn't sure I wanted to go into commercial piloting and certainly wasn't ready to settle down in a desk job."

"Are you glad this is what you chose?" she asked.

"I am. Every day is different, making it both rewarding and a challenge."

But nothing like today, she thought. Today had challenged and stretched them emotionally, and the scary thing was that it was far from over.

She glanced over at the hunky pilot sitting next to her. Her stepfather would like him. A lot. And in another life, Colton Landry was exactly the kind of man she would have liked to get to know better. Because she couldn't deny the attraction she felt toward the man. But anything more wasn't an option. She was focused on her own healing after her mother's death. Avoiding the complications of a relationship had seemed to be a wise decision in that process. Especially with the chance of things turning out the way her last relationship had.

She turned back to watch the colors of the sunset that continued to mute as darkness started to spread across the sky. "What do you find interesting about the desert?" she asked.

Before she'd even signed the contract to come, she'd been intrigued with North Africa, and she'd learned everything she could, not only about this country, but the desert, as well. She'd discovered it was one of the driest, and also one of the highest, places on Earth, where temperatures could easily reach over 130 degrees Fahrenheit and the total rainfall was less than three inches per year.

"Let's see… How about the fact that there are over forty species of rodents?"

"Rodents?" Lexi wrinkled her nose, then laughed. "I ask you about the beauty of this place, and you give me rodents?"

"I'm sorry. How about this? The Sahara's one of the most unique, diverse and yet beautiful places you'll ever see. Life for those who live here is slow paced, and hasn't changed for centuries. There are nomads, camels, colorful markets, small towns emerging from the earth like desert castles…"

He shot her that smile again. One that managed to jar her heart. She searched for a way to ignore it.

"I just wish…" She turned away from his gaze. "I wish circumstances were different right now. That my family wasn't worrying…"

"We're going to find a way out of this," he said.

She felt her chest constrict. "Don't make promises you can't keep. Even *Casablanca* didn't have a perfect happily-ever-after ending."

He wiped away a tear from her cheek with his thumb. "I've been in worse situations and made it out alive."

"You're kidding me, right?"

"An ambush by Iraqi insurgents during the war." His voice darkened. "I never thought I'd make it out of there."

"What happened?"

"I think I'll save that story for after we've been rescued and we're all safe and sound."

She couldn't help but smile at the thought of seeing him again, but even that crazy anticipation wasn't enough to dwarf the reality of the danger they faced. The monotony of the desert seemed to go on forever. No landmarks. Just the endless rise after shallow rise of darkening sand.

A shout from behind them pulled Lexi from her thoughts. She turned around and saw Bret running in their direction with a look of terror on his face.

She jumped up beside Colton. "Bret..."

He was stumbling toward them as fast as he could on the uneven sand. Even in the fading glow of the sunset, she could see his chest heaving, and tears running down his cheeks.

Colton grabbed Bret's arm to steady him. "What happened?"

"I don't know." Bret was gasping for breath as he slid down onto the sand in front of them and jerked up his pant leg. "Something...something stung me. But the pain... I think I'm going to pass out."

Colton knelt down beside him and looked at the spot just above his ankle. The site was already red and swelling.

"Did you see what it was?" he asked.

"Yeah... It...it looked like a scorpion."

"Can you describe it?" Colton asked.

"It was...I don't know...three, maybe four inches. And a strange color. Yellow, maybe green."

Colton drew in a sharp breath at the familiar description. If Bret really was describing a Deathstalker, it was one of the most toxic scorpions in the desert.

Can this day get any worse, God?

"Do you know what it was?" Lexi asked.

Colton shook his head. "I could be wrong, but I had

a coworker who was stung by a scorpion a few months ago, and his description sounds like what you're describing. It's called the Deathstalker, or sometimes the Israeli desert scorpion."

"How deadly is the sting?" Lexi asked.

"Reactions vary depending on the person." He didn't want to tell them that if he was right, it was extremely toxic. And with Bret's immune system already compromised...

"Well, the name Deathstalker doesn't sound encouraging," Bret said. He clenched his jaw then threw back his head.

"What's your pain level?" Colton asked.

"On a scale of one to ten? Off the charts," he said. "And I don't know if you remembered this, but I'm allergic to everything. Bees, wasps, fire ants—you name it."

Colton caught the fear in Bret's voice. That meant his risk of a serious reaction had just multiplied.

"Do you have an EpiPen?" Lexi asked.

"Yes..." He was rocking back and forth now, with sweat glistening across his forehead. "In the front pocket of my backpack. For some reason they let me keep it."

"Okay. I want you to stay here and try to stay calm." Colton stood up, then turned to Lexi. "I'll go grab the first aid kit and a couple blankets. You can get the EpiPen."

Lexi jogged beside him toward the plane. "What else do you know about this kind of scorpion?"

Colton hesitated a few seconds before answering. "From what I've heard, it doesn't normally do any permanent damage to a healthy adult. But not only is

Bret allergic to stings and bites, his immune system and health have been compromised over the past few weeks. Hopefully the EpiPen will counteract the fact that we don't have access to any antivenom."

Neither of them needed to state the obvious. In a best-case scenario, the swelling from a sting would subside after a day or two with no medical help. But if Bret had a severe reaction, this was an entirely different story. If the venom started moving rapidly through the body, his airways could be blocked. A reaction that could occur in a matter of minutes.

"And if the EpiPen isn't enough?" she asked before heading into the plane.

"Then we both better start praying harder."

Because in a few minutes any lingering light from the setting sun was going to vanish, to be replaced only by the white light of the moon. And striking out on their own across the desert looking for help in the middle of the Sahara at night wasn't an option.

This day just keeps getting worse and worse.

Colton hurried to where he'd stashed the first aid kit, trying not to think about how his sister was doing right now. He'd promised to get in touch as soon as he got to Morocco, which meant she was going to start wondering why he wasn't calling. And not only was he unable to reach her, he had no idea when he'd even have access to a phone.

At least he knew that her pastor was there with her, as well as their son, Noah. Bret's parents had booked a flight to Atlanta from Michigan, but they wouldn't get in for another few hours. He tried to push away the deepening worry for Bret and his family for now and forced his mind to focus on what they needed to do for him. And pray that what they were doing was going to be enough.

Grabbing the first aid kit and a couple blankets, he hurried back to the front of the plane, where he found Lexi holding the backpack and a bottle of water.

"Today hasn't turned out the way either of us expected, has it?" she said as they hurried back to where Bret was lying on the sand.

"No, it hasn't."

Darkness was slipping quickly across the desert, save the light of the moon that was rising in the night sky, as they knelt down beside Bret.

"How are you doing?" Colton pulled out the EpiPen from the front of the backpack. "Tell me what you're feeling."

Bret groaned. "Sick. Nauseated. It hurts so bad."

"I know. I need you to hang in there."

He sounded disoriented, and a check of his pulse confirmed that his heart was racing.

Colton removed the safety cap, then pushed the orange tip into Bret's thigh, while Lexi pulled out the cold pack and squeezed the bag to activate it.

"Will you grab a couple of the pain medicines from the kit and give those to him?" he asked.

Colton pressed the cold pack against the sting and continued praying.

Bret started shaking. "I'm sorry for getting you involved in this, Colton."

"Are you crazy?" he asked as Lexi helped him with the pain medicine. "You don't have anything to be sorry for."

"And you know what else? It's cold out here," Bret

said with a fake laugh. "We're in the middle of the Sahara, and I'm freezing."

"It's the effect of the adrenaline," Colton said. "You're going to be fine."

Bret's eyes rolled shut.

"Bret…" Colton grabbed his wrist to check his pulse. "His heart's racing. His breathing's rapid…"

"You're right," Lexi said, placing her arm on Colton's. "It's just the effect of the adrenaline."

Colton nodded. "I need you to take some deep breaths, Bret, and try and calm down."

Bret opened his eyes and nodded.

"Slow breaths, Bret. Slow breaths."

"I feel so sleepy now. Maybe if I sleep, I won't feel the pain anymore."

"You can sleep now. We're both going to be right here with you."

Lexi pulled him back a few steps and glanced up at him. "What if the EpiPen's not enough? I'm an engineer who can design a water system, but this—I don't know what else to do for him."

Colton caught the fear in her voice and wished he had the answer. "I don't either."

She pulled a second pen from the backpack. "If the first one doesn't clear up the symptoms, we can give him another dose."

"I agree, but I'm worried about him. His system's already weak from everything he's gone through. He needs proper medical attention." He felt his chest constrict.

"Come morning, do you think we can find our way out of here?"

"We don't have a choice anymore."

A swirl of dust formed in the distance in the fading sunlight. Lexi grasped his hand as it swirled higher.

Someone—or something—was coming.

FIVE

Lexi's heart pounded as a shadowy row of camels appeared over the moonlit ridge. She glanced at Colton as Bret's words played over in her mind. Either they were about to be rescued or their captors had found them.

"Stay here with Bret," Colton said, putting a protective arm in front of her. "I'll go see who they are."

She knelt back down beside Bret and started praying as she checked his pulse again. The redness from the sting had spread. He seemed restless and drowsy, and his heart was still racing.

Above them on the ridge, men in loose-fitting pants and long shirts climbed down from their camels. One of them started speaking loudly, his hands moving animatedly, but she couldn't understand what he was saying. Her gaze shifted to the rest of the group, and her breath caught. At least two of the men carried rifles.

"Who are they?" Bret asked.

She glanced down at Colton's brother-in-law. His face and neck were glistening with sweat. His breathing rapid...

"I don't know. Just try to stay calm and let Colton handle things."

But was that even possible? It seemed clear that whoever was after them wasn't going to stop because of a confrontation with the Malian army. They'd tried to escape, one of them had shot down their plane and chances were they were still looking for them.

No. This wasn't over yet.

What are we supposed to do, God? We've got people willing to kill us for what they want, not to mention Bret could die without medical attention...

"Lexi?"

Her heart pounded as Colton hurried down the hill toward them beside another man.

"Who are they?" she asked.

"Friends of mine. I want you to meet Issa."

"A friend of yours?" Lexi's gaze narrowed as she eyed the man standing next to Colton. He had a broad smile on his dark face, but she still wasn't ready to let down her guard.

"And the guns?" she asked. Her gaze shifted back to the two men standing on the ridge with their rifles.

Issa took a step toward her. "You must understand that not everyone who lives in this desert is willing to work for what they need. They wouldn't hesitate to take what we have by gunpoint. It is our only way to protect ourselves."

"It's okay, Lexi," Colton said. "I met Issa a few months ago during a medical evacuation of his wife and newborn son. Since then, he's become an invaluable resource for our team."

"Then I'm sorry for the cold welcome." A sigh of relief spread through her. "It's just that it's been a difficult day."

"Colton just told me about the kidnappings and the

plane crash. *That* was not the kind of welcome you deserved in my country. You have nothing to be sorry for," Issa said. "I'm simply happy that we can help."

"Issa received a message from my base," Colton said. "They realized from the GPS tracker that after crossing into Mauritania we must have had to make an emergency landing. They were able to get through to Issa and asked him to come find us."

"Then we're all grateful," Lexi said. She glanced over at Bret. "But we've got an even more serious problem right now."

"It's my brother-in-law. He was bitten by a scorpion," Colton said.

"And he's not getting any better." Lexi bit the edge of her lip to stop herself from crying. "I wanted to wait a few more minutes to see if the medicine would take effect, but he's going to need another shot, and after that…"

There was nothing else she could do.

"I will take you to the Kasbah where I live," Issa said, signaling to his men. "There is a woman there. A healer. She will know what to do."

Lexi glanced up the ridge at the row of camels. Above them, the Milky Way dangled beneath a black sky.

She'd seen photos of a Kasbah. Fortresses, often built on hilltops in order to be more easily defended, with high walls and no windows. At least she'd feel safer there than out here in the open in the middle of the desert.

Issa turned back to Colton. "There is an airstrip—not more than three hours farther—where your team can land and pick you up in the morning."

Colton nodded. "Thank you."

"You are welcome, but if we are going to help him, we need to hurry."

Any romantic ideas of riding a camel across the desert had been stripped away in the first twenty minutes of the trip. Each one of the camels was tethered to the tail of the one in front of them by some kind of halter, and together they moved at a slow but steady gait across the desert sands. If an hour on a horse could make her sore, she didn't even want to imagine what she was going to feel like come morning. And on top of that, the stench of the camels was only outdone by their constant spitting.

They'd put Bret on a makeshift stretcher behind her on one of the camels. Not that there was really anything she could do. Which was what had her worried. Because while she was trying to acclimate to the bumpy camel ride, Bret was getting worse.

She glanced up at the stars and forced herself to draw in a deep breath as she studied the expanse. A shooting star fled across the horizon, the distant red flicker of Mars, the Big Dipper and the expansive Milky Way hovering above them, so close it made her want to reach out and hold on to all of it.

And yet her entire experience in Africa so far had turned out to be one of letting go. Letting go of her own expectations in order to see not only those around her, but to discover what God wanted her to get out of her time here. Every morning when she woke up, she begged God not only to use her, but to give her strength to be able to handle what she would see that day. In a place where most people lived below the international poverty line, and where limited access to clean water meant higher rates of waterborne illnesses and child mortality, the pain she encountered was often devastating. And like tonight, she often felt too small and alone.

"How are you doing?" Colton's voice pulled her out of her thoughts.

He was walking beside her on the sand, keeping up with the steady gait of the camels.

A wave of emotion shot through her. The man she'd struggled to get out of her dreams had become her hero today. "I'm thinking you were the smart one, deciding to walk instead of ride one of these animals."

He grinned up at her in the moonlight. "I learned from experience. Tried it once and was sore for days afterward. I decided then if I was given the choice between walking and riding a camel, I'd been happy to walk."

Surrounded by endless sands drenched in moonlight and stardust, she couldn't help but smile. But as much as she might want to get to know the man who'd unexpectedly been thrust back into her life, this wasn't exactly the romantic scenario she'd dreamed about. The stakes were far too high.

She glanced back down at Colton, hesitating before voicing the question she'd been asking herself ever since the plane went down. Because she wasn't sure she wanted to know the answer. "Do you think they're still out there looking for us?"

"Honestly? I don't think we can ignore the possibility or assume they cannot reach this far. But I trust Issa. If anyone can get us to safety, he can."

She hoped he was right. Prayed he was right. Prayed even more that they wouldn't have to find out.

"What about Bret?"

Colton let out a sharp sigh. "The second dose of adrenaline seems to be helping, but not much. He's still struggling to breathe."

"I don't know what else to do except pray."

"I just finished speaking with Issa. He told me we're less than an hour from the Kasbah."

She just hoped that an hour wouldn't be too long for Bret to hold on.

"Colton?"

Lexi glanced down the long row of camels that were merely shadows beneath the night sky. Issa was running toward them.

"I need the three of you to come with me now. Quickly. My scouts have discovered men up ahead coming toward us. Until we can identify who they are, we need to hide you. There's a ridge just south of here. Between that and the cover of darkness you should be safe."

Lexi's heart pounded. The men who had kidnapped her had weapons that could knock a plane out of the sky and would be no match for the rifles Issa and his team carried. If they found them here...

"Hurry. We'll get your brother, but we don't have much time."

She used the saddle handles to push herself up, then swung her leg over the hump to one side. Colton took her hands to keep her steady while she found her balance. Then without hesitating, he laced their fingers together and ushered her toward the ridge into the darkness.

Colton could see the armed men from where he lay on the crest of the sand between Lexi and Bret. He wasn't sure that the description of the small rogue band of work-for-hire fighters the Malian army had given him was accurate either. They had to have a network reaching across the desert and across borders.

He needed to get both Bret and Lexi to a place where they could catch flights back to the States. But for the moment, that wasn't an option. They were miles away from any transport—other than camels—and just as far away from the medical help they needed.

He squeezed Lexi's hand as they watched the men who'd just arrived slowly walk down the long, tethered line of camels. Each one carried a weapon across his shoulder, and there was no doubt in his mind what they were looking for. Some of their men had been killed by the army; they'd just lost out on two million dollars, and that didn't include the money they wanted from Lexi's brother.

Knowing how scared she must be, Colton rubbed the back of her hand with his thumb, hoping to reassure her. But she wasn't the only one whose nerves were on edge. He'd calculated the risks when he'd agreed on the army's plan. Knew that his decision could cost him everything, including the life of his brother-in-law. And he'd decided it was a risk he couldn't afford not to take.

But Lexi's involvement in this situation had been far from voluntary. She'd come to Mali to make a difference in people's lives. And instead, she'd been taken hostage by a band of rogue militants. Not that life was always fair or just. He hadn't been kidding about being in a worse situation when he mentioned the ambush by the insurgents in Iraq. He'd been prepared to die that day.

He glanced down at her in the darkness, just able to

see the outline of her profile, unable to shake the strong desire to protect her and keep her safe. They needed to get out of here without getting caught.

Five minutes later, the men disappeared into the darkness. Issa made his way up the ridge to where they were.

"They found the crash site," Issa said.

Colton glanced at Lexi. "Then they know we're alive."

"Yes, but they are gone for now. I told them we heard of three Americans who were heading east."

"Which is the wrong direction." Colton glanced out into the darkness, then helped Lexi up. "Do you think they believed you?"

"I think so, but we need to hurry to the Kasbah. And make sure one of them does not follow us in the meantime."

"Do you want to ride again?" Colton asked, turning to Lexi.

"I'm fine. I'll walk for now."

The men settled Bret back into the makeshift stretcher, and the long line of camels were on their way again. This time, though, Colton's senses were on full alert. Every movement, every shadow in the distance could potentially be one of the men who'd come after them.

"I don't think you have told me the entire story, my friend," Issa said, stepping up beside them. "You said some men might be after your brother, and that he was kidnapped, but what exactly happened?"

"I was hoping you wouldn't have to get involved in this," Colton said.

"I already am involved. And as I said before, I want

to help. You saved the life of my son, which means I owe you mine."

"Tell him, Colton," Lexi said, keeping up beside them. "We can't do this on our own."

Colton frowned. He hadn't expected this unsanctioned mission to be easy. In fact, quite the opposite. He'd played out the scenario of rescuing Bret from every possible angle. And yet today had thrown two more potentially deadly scenarios at him. A plane crash. A scorpion bite. Neither had he imagined there would be more than one hostage to free. And now he had involved Issa and his men in the escape from a band of ruthless men.

"She's right, Colton," Issa said. "I cannot help stop what I do not understand."

Colton nodded. They were both right. This wasn't something he was going to be able to finish on his own. "Almost two months ago, my brother-in-law was visiting me on a mission trip. He's owns a construction business and was involved in building a hospital in Mali. A week after he arrived, he was taken for ransom. Those behind the kidnapping demanded two million dollars."

"I heard about the kidnapping, but didn't know he was your relative."

"Bret's business does well, but to come up with two million dollars wasn't possible. Instead, I struck a deal with the Malian army. I was to go in with two suitcases filled with counterfeit money for the exchange. The army was supposed to take care of the rest."

"But they didn't?"

"No. They were there as promised, but apparently the network is far more extensive than they thought.

We got away, but they managed to shoot down our plane, and now they are still searching for us. Even here across the border."

"They are not happy that their payment got away," Issa said. "Two million dollars would go a long way to fund their organization."

"And you?" he said, turning to Lexi. "How do you fit into this?"

"My brother owes some man a large sum of money. Trent can't be located, so I was taken in order to get to him."

"Do you know where your brother is?"

She shook her head. "He was in Mali for a while, then left without telling me where he was going. I haven't heard from him since."

"All three of you need to leave the country as soon as possible," Issa said. "And the safest place I believe is on to Morocco. Because I think I know who might have taken your brother-in-law. His name is Salif."

"Who is he?" Colton asked. "A terrorist?"

Issa shook his head. "Salif is no terrorist. More of an opportunist. He makes his money doing work-for-hire for extremist organizations and kidnapping tourists, among other dishonorable things."

"Do you think he survived the army's attack?"

"He has men working under him. I doubt he was even there. Which means all we know for sure is that there is a large amount of money at stake and someone is willing to do anything to get it back."

"So what do you think we should do in the mean-time?" Colton asked.

"I will warn my men to keep quiet about your pres-ence. We might be out in the middle of nowhere, but you'd be surprised how fast news travels. And don't worry about your brother-in-law. We are close now. In fact, you can see the outline of the Kasbah just ahead."

Colton felt relief shoot through him at the sight of the Kasbah. The structure was built on high ground, then loomed toward the sky like a majestic stronghold. Arriving here meant they were that much closer to safety. By tomorrow afternoon they'd be in Morocco and out of reach of the men who wanted them. And his brother would be that much closer to being reunited with his family.

"It's beautiful," Lexi said.

"I agree," Issa said. "While I am used to a life of moving around in tents, I'm always happy to come home to a permanent structure like this."

"How old is it?" Colton asked.

"It was built over four centuries ago," Issa said. "There are rooms designed to get sun in the winter and not in the summer. Walls circle the small city. They were built originally for defensive purposes, but I promise you will appreciate the view in the daytime."

"And you're sure we'll be safe here?" Lexi asked.

Colton caught the fear in her eyes and wished he could guarantee her safety.

So many things are out of my control, God.

"I will do everything in my power to ensure just that," Issa said, breaking into his thoughts. "But the first thing we must do is look for Sara. She is the one who will help your brother-in-law."

A knot of dread grew in Colton's stomach. Issa was right. They needed to needed to leave the country as soon as possible. But in the meantime, all he could do was pray that the other men hadn't managed to follow them, and that Bret survived the night.

SIX

Lexi sat on one of the cushioned wooden benches and watched Colton while he paced the small courtyard near the room where Sara treated Bret. On any other night, the swaying potted palm trees, sand-colored walls and colorful rugs lit by a row of lanterns would have been inviting. Even the cool breeze blowing in from the desert across the open space was the perfect temperature. But not tonight. Instead the tangible tension hanging in the air had become an unrelenting reminder that they might have escaped Salif's men but their ordeal was not over.

Colton combed his fingers through his hair. "I keep thinking about how ironic it would be for Bret to survive being taken hostage in the middle of the Sahara by a group of insurgents only to die from a scorpion bite."

Lexi shifted her seat, wishing she could reassure him that everything would be okay. "Don't even go there, Colton—"

"I just wish I knew that he was going to survive this." He stopped in front of her and caught her gaze in the yellow glow of the lanterns. "Becca—his wife— didn't want him to come here. She was afraid something was going to happen to him. I just kept telling her to stop worrying. And then all of this happened."

"And you somehow feel that it's your fault," she said, stating the obvious.

"Yes—"

"But it's not." She stood up in front of him and brushed her fingers against his forearm. "You didn't cause any of this. If anything, you're the hero. If you hadn't risked your life to save Bret today, there's no telling what those men would have done to him. To both of us."

She could see the lingering reflection of guilt in his eyes. But it was more than that. The stress of the past few weeks were evident from the deep, furrowed lines across his forehead and the slight tinge of gray showing at his temple. Whether it was his fault or not, he clearly felt responsible.

He shoved his hands into his front pockets and shrugged. "Maybe you're right, but I was the one who convinced him to come. My sister hates to travel, but Bret had always wanted to come to Africa. And for me...I wanted someone in my family to see where I was working and get a feeling of what it was like here on a day-to-day basis. I just never expected things to turn out like this."

"That's the thing. None of us ever expects tragedy. But even knowing that things *do* go wrong sometimes doesn't mean we hide from life. Look at your own life. You haven't exactly done that by coming here. And as for Bret, he could have been in a car wreck back home, or injured in a construction accident..."

His jaw tensed and he started pacing again. "Maybe, but I also know how hard this ordeal has been for Becca and Noah. If I don't end up bringing him home now after everything he's gone through…"

The wooden door behind them creaked open, pausing their conversation. A woman wearing a loose traditional dress in bright oranges and reds opened the door and motioned for them to come inside.

Lexi stepped inside behind Colton, then glanced around the room at the yellow painted walls. There were large windows, to catch the breeze she imagined, and large, colorful rugs on the tiled floor. The ceilings—built with several wooden beams—were at least seven feet tall. Bret lay sleeping on a bed in the middle of the room beneath a mosquito net that had been tied back. The only light came from two lanterns hanging beside the bed that left dark shadows in the corners of the room.

"How is he?" Colton asked, stepping beside the bed.

"Very weak, but his breathing is more regular, and I believe the pain has lessened. He finally fell asleep a few minutes ago."

"So he's going to be all right?"

She nodded. "He will need to rest and eat to gain his strength, but yes, there is no reason to believe he won't recover completely."

"What did you give him?" Colton asked.

Sara picked up a gourd the size of a small melon from a worn basket on the floor next to the bed. "It's milky sap is often used by my people to treat scorpion bites."

"What's it called?" Lexi took the offered gourd from the woman and held it up to the light in front of her.

"We call it Alkhad. It is a desert plant. You can't eat it, but it is good for healing and cleansing of the body."

Lexi ran her fingers across the rough surface of the gourd, then handed it back to the older woman, curious to know more. But it wasn't as if she could Google the name. Somehow the thought made her chuckle. Here they were in the middle of the Sahara, miles from any major town. The whole situation just seemed so unreal. Which was why laughing seemed better than crying.

Sara dropped the gourd back into the basket, then turned to Colton. "Issa told me he was taken by one of Salif's men."

"That's who Issa believes is responsible. They kept him captive for almost two months."

"That explains in part why he reacted more severely to the sting. His body is weaker than most. It is also why he needs rest. He will need to stay here for a few days in order for him to gain his strength back."

Colton glanced at Lexi. "I'm not sure we can do that. We need to leave the country as soon as possible. Salif's men are out there looking for us."

Sara didn't look convinced. "It would not be safe for him to travel. I've also given him something to help with the pain and to ensure he sleeps, but his body needs rest."

"What can we do to help Bret in the meantime?" Lexi asked. They would have to discuss their options, but no one was going anywhere tonight.

"Get some rest yourselves," she said. "I will stay with him tonight, though it is unlikely he will wake up. In the morning, I will have some rice and meat sauce prepared for when he wakes up. He should eat a small amount at first, slowly increasing. And he needs to drink, as well. In a few days, once his strength has begun to return, he should be ready to leave."

In a few days?

She caught the shadow that crossed Colton's face. What if they didn't have a few days? What if Salif's men managed to track them down here at the Kasbah or on the way to meet the plane?

Lexi turned around as Issa slipped into the room behind them. "How is he?"

"Still weak," Colton said, "but Sara believes he will be fine after a few days of rest."

"I knew Sara could help. Her traditional healing practices are known throughout the region." Issa turned to Lexi. "And how are you feeling?"

"Tired, yet relieved to be here."

Relieved to finally be safe.

She wondered how much time had passed since they'd snatched her. Thirty, forty hours? It seemed more like a blur of days instead. And as far as she knew, her family had no idea she'd been taken by Salif's men. Her best friend Micah had to be wondering why she wasn't answering her emails. With Micah's wedding in less than a week, she knew her friend was probably wondering why she hadn't heard from her. And then there was Trent. She had no idea where her brother was or if he had any intention of coming forward to the men who'd taken her.

"I have explained to them that he is too weak to travel," Sara said.

Issa's frown deepened. "I understand your concerns, Sara, and the three of you are welcome to stay as long as you need, but if Salif or his men were to try and search here...I'm not sure we could keep you safe."

"Which is why we need to leave the country." Colton turned to Lexi. "What do you think?"

She bit her lip, mulling over their limited options. "I agree that it doesn't seem wise to stay here. Not when we know they are still looking for us. If your team could pick us up tomorrow, we could wait in Morocco a few days for him to recover."

Issa nodded. "It's a good option and probably less of a risk than staying here."

"And while we're there, I can try to track down Trent."

Lexi hesitated at the comment. She'd purposely avoided dwelling on what her brother had supposedly done. Maybe it was partly because she still didn't want to believe he'd knowingly put her in danger by coming to stay with her—causing her capture. But in her heart, she knew it was true. Which was why she needed to find him and make sure he made things right with the men after him. Surely someone at the embassy would have contacts and could check to see where he'd flown out of in the last forty-eight hours. Of course if he was running, he was going to be doing everything possible not to be found.

Colton caught the flicker of pain in Lexi's expression. Bret had been abducted by strangers, but she'd been betrayed by her own brother. If a reunion with Trent did take place, it was going to be anything but happy.

"Lexi?" he said. "I know this is a different situation you're facing with your brother—"

"I'm okay." She nodded her head and lifted her chin slightly. "I'd rather not think about Trent right now. We just need to concentrate on making sure Bret gets well, and that we all get to safety. I'll deal with what my brother did as soon as I can find him."

"She's right, Colton." Issa clasped Colton's forearm. "There's really nothing more any of us can do here. Sara will stay with him while my wife has dinner prepared for us. So come with me. I'll take you up to our apartment now."

Colton and Lexi followed Issa through the darkened maze of tiny medieval passageways. With only a few lanterns and the light of the moon to guide their way along the uneven ground, they passed by whitewashed walls that were painted halfway up in a deep blue.

"A person could get lost in here," Colton said as they took yet another turn.

"Kasbahs were originally built to be fortified cities. An enemy, even if he could breach the walls or perhaps one of the heavy wooden doors, would quickly get confused."

"How long has your family lived here?" Lexi asked.

"I am the fourth generation. My great-grandfather lived here with his wives—

"Wives?" Lexi asked. "How many did he have?"

"I'm not even sure how many there were, but the long, narrow passages and dozens of rooms were built to do more than just keep out an adversary. It was also to keep all the wives separated," Issa said. "I'm sure you can imagine what it was like for a man to have numerous families. Apparently it caused less problems if they didn't have to see each other."

Colton chuckled at the thought. As far as he was concerned, one wife was plenty. In fact, he found it hard to imagine how any man would even want to deal with more than one woman.

Not that he was interested in finding a wife.

He glanced at Lexi, who was keeping up beside him, clearly trying to take in everything around her. He ducked as Isaa led them up a windy, steep staircase that led to a flat roof and the smell of simmering vegetables and meat.

"This is where I live with my family. In the daytime, you can watch the desert for miles. Tonight it's the stars that seem to go on forever," Issa said.

"Wow." Lexi walked to the half wall surrounding the space. He watched the wind blowing through her hair as she looked up at the sky and the brilliance of God's masterpiece. "This is beautiful."

"The meal is almost ready, but first I have something for you." He picked up a small black box sitting in a cushioned alcove. "I thought you might want to call your family."

"A satellite phone?" Lexi turned around.

"Surprised?" Issa asked.

"I admit I assumed we were too remote for things like this. Even in the city where I've been living, cell phone service is spotty at best in some of the places where I work."

"It's solar powered," Issa said, "which means you can use it just about anywhere. And while there have been a few times when the atmosphere interferes with the reception, I've never been without service for long. You'd be amazed at how we are able to keep up with technology out here. Satellite television, phones. Last year I even joined Facebook."

"I can't tell you how grateful we are for your help," Colton said, taking the phone and turning to Lexi. "Why don't you call your father first? Even assuming he doesn't know what has happened, you can let him know you're well."

She smiled at him as she took the phone, but he didn't miss the shadow that crossed her face. Telling her father what had happened, along with the fact that her stepbrother was missing, wasn't going to be easy.

"Dad..." she said, once the call had gone through. "It's Lexi."

Colton moved to the other side of the roof with Issa to give her some privacy.

"She's a beautiful woman, though I'm assuming you already noticed?"

Colton looked up at the stars that seemed close enough to reach out and grab, surprised at Issa's forwardness. "Yes."

"You do know that a good woman is worth more than a hundred camels, don't you?" Issa asked.

"Is that one of your tribe's proverbs?" Colton asked, resting his elbows against the ledge and smiling at the comparison.

"No. Just what I've learned from experience. A wife who can cook a mouthwatering stew, keep her tongue from speaking lies and survive hardships by your side is worth her weight in gold, as I believe the English expression goes. Either way, I think for you, it would be hard to find a woman better than Lexi."

"I barely know her," Colton said, still grinning.

"That is true, but a woman who leaves her home and travels in order to help others must have an extraordinary heart. Besides that, it would seem that the two of you have quite a few things in common."

He couldn't argue, except he wasn't looking for a relationship. He glanced across the rooftop to where she was talking animatedly. Of course if he were looking, he'd definitely want someone like Lexi.

"Colton?"

Lexi walked toward him. He shook off the attraction he admittedly felt. Hadn't he learned his lesson with Maggie?

"Did your father know?" he asked.

She nodded. "One of my coworkers who saw me taken called him a few hours ago and told him what had happened. But of course the details were sketchy and no one really knew what had happened. To say that he was relieved to hear my voice is an understatement."

Her hands shook as she gave him the phone.

"Are you okay?" he asked, catching her gaze.

She clenched her fingers tight and pulled her hands against her sides. "Yeah, I guess… It's just that when I told him what happened it seemed so real. And on top of that, I suppose, it made me realize how fortunate I am that I'm here and alive."

"I can't stop thinking about that, as well. Despite all the continuing issues."

He felt again the urge to pull her into his arms and tell her that she was okay. That he was going to do everything in his power to make sure that the men who took her never had a chance to come near her again. Instead he took a step back and drew in a deep breath.

"He promised to get in touch with my coworkers and let them know I'm okay," she said.

"And your brother?" Colton asked, wondering if he should broach the subject. "Has he heard from him?"

She shook her head. "Not in several days. He has no idea where he might be."

"Okay. Then I'll call Becca and let her know what's going on."

Colton dialed his sister's number, then waited for the call to go through. He glanced out across the endless sea of desert beneath the moonlight. It was remarkable he was able to even make this phone call. Especially since this was the moment he'd been praying for the past few weeks. The chance to call Becca and tell her that the nightmare was almost over.

"Hello?"

"Becca, it's Colton. I'm still in Africa…" There was static on the line. "Can you hear me?"

"Yes… Colton…but Bret—"

"I'm with him now," Colton said, debating how much information to give Becca.

"He's with you?"

"The plan worked. He's safe."

All she really needed to know was that Bret was alive and going to be all right. Everything else—the plane crash, the scorpion sting and the fact that the men who took him were still out there looking for him— would only make her worry more. "Long story short, we're at a Kasbah in the middle of the desert, planning to fly out in the morning."

"I thought you were flying straight to Morocco today?" she asked.

"There have been a few…complications, which means it might take us a day or two longer to get home, but we're on our way."

Even with the static he could tell she was crying. "Becca, what's wrong?"

There was a long pause on the line.

"What if he's still not safe? What if Noah and I aren't safe?"

"I don't understand. What are you talking about?"

"I received a phone call a couple hours ago from the same men who first demanded the ransom. The two million dollars they asked for…they still want it. And if they don't get it in the next forty-eight hours they threatened to come after Noah and I here in the States."

SEVEN

Becca's words slammed into Colton's gut. Salif was threatening to come after her and Noah? How was that even possible? His call had to be nothing more than empty threats. There was no way they could reach Becca in the United States.

Or was there?

"Where are you now?" he asked, his mind still trying to work through the consequences of what she'd just told him.

"We're both at my parents' home, along with Bret's mom and dad, but I'm not sure we're safe here, and I can't put our parents' lives at risk. I'm thinking about disappearing for a few days with Noah."

Colton started pacing again. He'd obviously considered the current risk to Bret while they were still in North Africa, but this...

"Have you gone to the police?" he asked.

"They said they still had Bret and told me not to go to the authorities—"

"You need to get the authorities involved."

"I know. That's what I decided. I called Agent Salem."

"And?"

"He pretty much said there was nothing he could do. He said he'd look into the situation, but didn't see how a threat like that could be credible. Maybe he's right, but they knew my cell phone number, where I work, where Noah goes to school..."

"Most of these things they could have found out on Facebook. It could be nothing more than empty threats—"

"Empty threats?" She was crying again. "They held Bret hostage for almost two months. That's not an empty threat. You might have pulled him out of there, but what if this isn't over?"

"We have a plan, Becca. My team is going to fly in and pick us up in the morning. We'll go straight to Morocco, then catch a flight out from there. I'll let you know as soon as I can when we'll be back home."

He'd planned to have her fly to Morocco to meet them, but with threats against her and Noah, he wanted to keep them as far away from here as possible.

"Okay, but in the meantime, how is Bret doing physically? I know he needs to see a doctor. His immune system had to have been compromised. And he's likely malnourished and dehydrated after all these weeks in captivity."

"He's weak," Colton said, deciding not to mention the scorpion sting, "but he's going to be okay. We're somewhere safe right now, and tomorrow my team will pick us up. If everything goes according to plan, we'll be in Morocco by nightfall tomorrow, then I'll get Bret on a flight to the States. I promise, Becca. He's going to be okay. Trust me. I'm going to do everything in my power to ensure his safety and bring him home to you."

But in the meantime he now had to worry about his sister and Noah, as well.

He cleared his throat. "Maybe you're right about finding a place off the grid. I don't think they can reach you where you are, but if there is even a chance that they can make good on their threats we don't want to take it."

"I agree. I took a bunch of cash out of the ATM. I can head up the coast and find us a place to stay in some little seaside town where no one can find us."

"I think that's a good idea," he said. "But I'm going to need a way to contact you."

"I'm one step ahead of you. I'm ditching this phone now that I've heard from you, but I bought one of those burn phones that can't be traced."

"You've been watching way too many episodes of *NCIS*."

Becca let out a low chuckle, but he could still hear the fear in her voice. "Just write down the number."

"Just a sec..." He signaled at Issa for something to write with, then wrote the number on the back of his hand until he could find some paper.

"I'm not taking any more chances, Colton. Not with my son. Call me as soon as you're in Morocco and as soon as you know when you'll be back in the States."

"I will, and, little sis, be careful."

Seconds later the line went dead.

Lexi walked up to him and brushed her fingers against his arm. "What's going on? That didn't sound like the phone call you expected."

"It wasn't." Colton took a deep breath, still trying to wrap his mind around what his sister had just told him. And whether or not the threats were worth taking seriously. "Becca received a call from someone a few hours ago and the person on the other line threatened her and Noah's life if he didn't get the two million dollars they were supposed to get as Bret's ransom. Said they would come after them next if they didn't pay it in the next forty-eight hours."

"Wait a minute..." Lexi turned to Isaa. "Do you think there is any validity to their threat?"

Issa shook his head. "It's hard to imagine that their arm reaches all the way to the United States, but on the other hand we can't just assume they are bluffing."

"What about the police?" Lexi asked. "Aren't they involved?"

"They threatened to kill her and my nephew if they went to the police. But my sister has contacted the agent who was helping us with the case before. He's promised to look into the situation, I'm just not sure there's much he can do."

"I'm so sorry."

"I need to get Bret home. I need to be there with my sister and make sure she's okay." Colton turned to Issa. "And I need to know more about the man you mentioned. Salif. What exactly are we dealing with?"

"He was born and raised in Mali. Joined the army at some point, then decided that kidnapping would be more lucrative. There are men who hire Salif to do their dirty work as I told you earlier. Salif, in turn, has men who work under him, but no one knows exactly how many."

"So how far does this man's arm reach?"

"I can't be certain. I thought getting you to Morocco would be far enough. It's possible he has support in the United States, but I doubt it. I just have no way to know," Issa said, motioning them toward a small table. "In the meantime, the two of you need to eat. My wife has prepared a meal for you."

Issa's wife, a beautiful woman with dark skin and white teeth, carried out a large silver tray covered with an assortment of dishes.

"Colton, you remember my wife, Maysa?"

"Of course. It's a pleasure to see you again, Maysa," he said, then quickly introduced Lexi.

Issa's wife place the tray in front of them, then began pulling off the lids, intensifying the scents of cumin, garlic and onions. But any appetite he'd had was gone.

"You must eat, my friend," Issa said after blessing the food. He seemed to sense Colton's hesitation.

"He's right," Lexi said. "And it looks delicious. What is it?"

"We call this tagine," Issa said, pointing to one of the dishes beside a pile of flat bread. "It has fish, spices, olives and potatoes with couscous. There are also figs and grapes."

Colton picked up a piece of the flat bread, scooped up some of the sauce and took a bite. His mouth watered. Perhaps he was hungry after all. "I haven't had a chance to ask your husband about your son," he said, addressing Maysa.

Her face beamed with joy. "He is sleeping now, but he is...perfect."

"They almost lost the baby during the delivery," Colton said. "I was able to transport him to one of our clinics."

"If you will excuse me for a few minutes," Maysa said, standing up, "I will return with some tea and almond cakes."

"Thank you." Colton scooped up another bite of the sauce. "I didn't think I was hungry, but now that I've taken a bite I'm suddenly famished."

A star shot across the night sky above them. But even the warmth of the food wasn't enough to lessen the cold fear circulating through his heart.

An hour later, Colton tried unsuccessfully to sleep. The breeze coming in from the open window helped keep the room from being hot and stuffy. With dreams eluding him, he decided to talk to God.

How did the escape plan work only to lead us here, God? With threats now against Becca and Noah I don't know what to do. I need You to show me what to do.

He was worried about his sister and nephew. About Bret. And then there was Lexi. He'd been surprised at her strength throughout this entire ordeal. She was so different from Maggie. Maggie would never have taken a year off and come to Africa to serve others. It made him wonder now why he'd been attracted to her in the first place. Or maybe he was the one who had changed. He hadn't expected his decision to come to Africa to have made such a profound effect on his life. But it had. Of course, on the other hand, his brother-in-law never would have been captured by a group if militants if he'd never come in the first place.

But then he never would have met Lexi.

He couldn't help smiling when he pictured her. He liked her independence, and yet there was that underlying sense of vulnerability that made him want to protect her.

But what if I can't, God? All of this seems so out of my control.

It was what he'd always loved about flying. That feeling of control he felt when he was in the cockpit. But now with everything that had happened, he'd been reminded that he never really had been in charge.

A sharp knock on his door jerked him from his thoughts.

"Colton, come." Issa stood in the doorway. "We must hurry."

He leaned up on one elbow and waited for his eyes to focus. "Issa—"

"A group of armed men have just arrived at the Kasbah. And they are looking for you. My brother tried to convince them you weren't here, but they insisted on searching. And there is no way to stop them."

The sound of a familiar voice jerked Lexi out of her nightmare, but not enough for her to forget the dream. A group of armed men had been chasing her through the desert. And no matter how hard she pushed herself, it had been as if she'd been moving in slow motion as she struggled to make her way across the sand. She'd glanced behind her, but they'd continued to gain on her. In a few more seconds they would have been close enough to grab her.

The voice was calling her again. Fear swept over her as she tried to remember where she was. This wasn't just a dream. They had grabbed her and taken her into the desert. The only reason she had escaped was because of Colton.

"Lexi?"

This time she opened her eyes and looked up. Moonlight filtered through the window. Colton was leaning over her, his hand on her shoulder, shaking her gently. Her mind flashed back to the moment she'd first seen him at the camp. Before the guns started exploding around them. Somehow he'd managed to get her to safety.

"Lexi...we need to go. Quickly."

"Go where?" She fought to shake off the fog that had settled on her brain as she tried to take in his words. "I don't understand."

"The men who were looking for us have just arrived at the Kasbah."

Lexi felt her heart pound inside her chest. Her kidnappers were here? A wave of panic streaked through her. No...they couldn't have found them. Issa had sent them off in the wrong direction. And besides, this Kasbah was supposed to be a place of safety. She couldn't go back.

"We're going to be okay, but I need you to come with me now."

Lexi nodded, then sat up and brushed her hair back from her face, as the reality of their situation grabbed hold. They weren't safe. Not yet. Colton might have pulled her from Salif's camp, but those had taken her were not done searching for them yet. And if they really were here...

She looked around the room, but she had nothing to grab and take with her. No passports. No bags. She had no idea how they'd eventually cross the border without documents, but at the moment it didn't matter. They just needed to get as far away as possible from her abductors were determined to track them down.

Colton grabbed her hand and helped her up. "You okay?"

She nodded. "Just groggy. Where's Bret?"

"A couple of Issa's men have taken him to one of the Jeeps. We're going to meet him there, then leave the Kasbah."

Issa was waiting for them in the long, narrow passageway. "Come, we must hurry. My brother tried to hold them off, but they have guns."

"How many are there?" Colton asked as they followed Issa.

"I'm not sure. Five...maybe six. They arrived in a vehicle about ten minutes ago."

"I knew we never should have involved you and put your family at risk," Colton said.

"Forget it. I don't want to see Salif succeed any more than you do. Ransom payments give him the funds for weapons, and those in turn are used against my people."

They were winding their way through the dark maze of tiny passageways inside the Kasbah. Lexi could hear men shouting behind them as they ran. Her heart pounded in her throat as they made their way across the uneven brick. She tripped on a crack in the pavement. Colton grasped her elbow to stop her from falling.

"I'm fine," she said, ignoring the pain shooting through her ankle. "We need to keep going."

The men's footsteps behind them were getting louder.

"Through here," Issa said.

He unlatched a heavy wooden door and ushered them inside a small room with no ceiling that was open to the night sky. Lexi breathed in the musty smell of animals and constant bleating. Something brushed across her leg and pushed her backward against the wall.

"What in the world..."

"Sorry. They're sheep."

Sheep? He had to be kidding.

Moonlight caught the bodies of the animals that filled the room. In any other situation she'd see the humor in the situation. A room filled with sheep in a Kasbah in the middle of the desert… But right now, it was all she could do not to panic.

Issa was making his way in front of them, through another door and this time down another narrow staircase.

"I told you my grandfather had a number of wives," Issa said, his breathing fast. "He used these passageways to discreetly visit them. When I was a child, I would hide from my brothers and sisters using these tunnels. We're almost there."

Lexi glanced back as Colton grasped her hand and led her around a sharp twist in the flight of stairs. Her lungs were burning. The light of the moon had vanished, and the dark stone walls began to close in on her. She pressed her fingers against the cold rock.

God, this is not the time for me to be claustrophobic.

"Lexi?"

"It's nothing. I'm fine."

Colton squeezed her hand. "Just breathe slowly. We're almost there."

She drew in a breath. In and out, wishing she wasn't so terrified. When she'd agreed to take the job in Timbuktu, she'd been fully aware of the unpredictable security situation and the threat of kidnapping and terrorism. She'd seen the heavy security presence of police patrols. She—along with her team—had lived with contingency plans to leave the country on short notice if necessary. And now she was having to escape in the middle of the night from men who wanted to take her again.

Lexi drew in another deep breath, as they rushed down the narrow passageway. Despite the fear she felt, she wanted to believe that coming here had been worth it. That she'd do it all over again given the choice.

Because she'd come to love this country and the strength of the women who would do anything to protect their children. Women who worked hard from sunup to sundown to provide for their families. And she'd found contentment in helping to ensure they had the clean water they needed to protect their families.

Now the contentment she'd found in her work had been exchanged for a growing sense of panic. Even if they did get out of here without being followed, where would they go? Salif clearly had men spread out over a vast territory. Yet how could they give in to his demands when they didn't have what he wanted?

Colton didn't have the two million dollars. She didn't know where her brother was or if he had access to the money he owed them.

Issa pushed open another heavy wooden door that opened up into some sort of garage, then let them pass.

"Here's the Jeep."

Two men were helping Bret into the front passenger seat. One of them grabbed a package off the top of the vehicle and handed it to Issa.

"Where do we go now?" Lexi asked, hesitating.

"We need to head for the boarder."

"What about my team?" Colton asked.

"I'm bringing the satellite phone. For them to land at this point isn't safe. Rumor has it that Salif's men are guarding all the airstrips in the vicinity."

"So we drive out of here?" Lexi asked.

"I believe it is our only option. I'll come with you as your driver. I know the way."

Issa handed Colton a weapon. "Just in case we need to defend ourselves. These men are heavily armed, which means it won't be enough to take them down, but at least it will give us some way to defend ourselves."

Lexi stared at the weapon and felt her stomach tighten as Issa put a second handgun beneath the driver's seat. She'd never liked guns, despite her stepfather's collection. And while she could agree there was a time and a place, she hated the fact that they might need one now.

"Lexi?"

"Sorry." She jumped into the backseat next to Colton and felt that eerie sense of déjà vu sweep over her. They'd tried to lose Salif's men before, and his men had found them. Which mean that while Issa might know the desert, so did these men. They'd grown up here. They knew how to survive in the stark conditions. And they knew how to be ruthless.

All *she* knew was that this was a world completely different from her own.

The fear was back, twisting in her gut. The night sky loomed above them as Issa sped away from the Kasbah. She glanced at Colton and caught the same look of worry in his eyes as he reached out and grasped her hand.

"We're going to get out of this."

She nodded, but wasn't convinced anymore that there was a way out.

EIGHT

Colton felt the strap of the shoulder belt catch, then pull tightly across his chest as Issa accelerated, leaving behind the confines of the Kasbah. The same seeds of alarm that had been planted when he'd first received his sister's call that Bret had been kidnapped had sprung to life again. Because this was far from over. Just when he'd thought his brother-in-law was safe, everything was—once again—crumbling down around them. And this time he wasn't sure he knew how to put an end to the continual nightmare.

Bracing one hand against the seat in front of him and the other on the armrest, he studied Lexi's grim expression as she sat in silence beside him. Like he'd told her, he'd been in situations where he'd been convinced there was no way out alive. Circumstances where comrades had lost their lives beside him, and that still haunted him. But there was one major difference in this situation. He and his fellow soldiers had trained in combat, expecting to encounter death. It was an inevitable risk of their job. And while it was something he'd prayed wouldn't happen, that possibility had always been there, lingering in the back of his mind. Today, though, it was the urgent sense of duty to bring his brother-in-law—and Lexi—home safe that had him focused.

He turned to look out the back window of the 4x4 to see if they were being followed. Visibility was limited. The sun had yet to make its appearance over the horizon, but rays of light were already spreading across the orange sand.

"Do you see them behind us?" Issa asked from the driver's seat.

"No, but that doesn't mean they're not back there." All he could see was the never-ending desert being bathed in the obscure yellow light of the sunrise. And the winds were strong enough that the dust didn't allow him to discern if there was a vehicle behind them.

Which would hopefully give them the same cover, as well.

"I'm not surprised," Issa said. "It's hard to see more than fifty meters ahead of us, and it's getting worse."

Something else to worry about. As well as Issa knew this desert, to be out here now with the winds picking up wasn't a wise choice. Sandstorms were common in this part of the world and could overcome a vehicle in a matter of seconds. But what other choice did they have?

He turned back to where Bret lay against the front passenger seat with his eyes closed. The jarring of the vehicle as it sped across the sand was anything but comfortable. This wasn't what Bret needed. He was supposed to be resting, not on the move, running for his life.

Colton leaned forward and grasped the injured man's shoulder. "Bret...are you okay?"

He just groaned and turned his head.

"Bret?"

Still he wouldn't answer.

Colton felt his forehead for signs of a fever, but he didn't seem hot. Only clammy.

Issa shifted gears as they went up a slight embankment. "When I spoke to Sara late last night she told me she'd given him something to help him sleep. I'm guessing it should wear off soon, but until then I suspect he's going to feel extremely groggy."

Colton sat back against his seat and gripped the armrest again.

What are we supposed to do, God? Take a risk and ask my team to meet at an airstrip or try to make it all the way to the border?

The airstrip was less than an hour away, and flying would get them to Morocco sooner, and it would avoid the long trip across the desert. But if Issa was right, if Salif's men were covering the surrounding airstrips, sending his team to meet them wasn't a chance he wanted to take. Which meant their only option was to lose the men who were after them and head for the border.

"You're worried." Lexi caught his gaze, her words more of a statement than a question.

"Issa knows this area better than most. If anyone can get us to safety, he can."

Colton frowned at his own words. What he said was true, but they'd somehow sounded hollow. Salif's men knew this desert, as well. And they clearly had resources that included weapons and the ability to shoot down a small plane out of the sky. Which meant that the four of them were outnumbered and outgunned. If the men who were after their group caught up with them…

He reached out and squeezed Lexi's hand a moment before letting go. "What about you? You okay?"

"I guess that's up for interpretation," she said, but he didn't miss the determination in her eyes. "Twenty-four hours or so ago, I was facing being held ransom for who knows how long. Now I'm speeding across the desert with a group of armed men closing in on us, and there doesn't seem to be anything I can do beyond pray that we'll make it out."

"I've been doing a lot of that lately. Praying. Sometimes it's hard to not wonder what lesson God might be trying to impart to me."

"Maybe He's just trying to teach you to rely on Him," she said. "That's what I keep coming back to. I've spent so much of my life trying to control situations, but living here the past few months has changed all of that. I've learned that I can't get around the red tape in this country. I can't fix every broken water system, or especially get things done quicker. And right now there's nothing I can do on my own to change any of this. Just hold on for dear life and trust."

He'd already come to admire that attitude. That determined set of her chin. The fact that despite being caught in a situation that would have most people in a complete panic, she had yet to allow fear to immobilize her.

He couldn't help the image of Maggie with her polished nails and red lips that surfaced in his mind. He wondered how she'd cope with a situation like this. Especially wearing one of the five-hundred-dollar suits she wore every day to the law firm she worked for. Which wasn't really a fair comparison. Maggie was smart and ambitious and had no qualms confronting an opponent head-on. But dealing with poverty, sickness and insurgents in the desert? Somehow law school didn't prepare you for this scenario.

Or maybe nothing could prepare you for this. Maybe it was nothing more than the circumstances they'd now been thrown into. Circumstances that forced each one of them to dig up every ounce of strength they had left.

"Just so you know, I'm speaking to myself more than to you," Lexi said, holding tight to the armrest as the 4x4 flew across the bumpy sand. "Trying to convince myself that somehow this is all going to end up okay."

The wind was blowing sand through the cracks and crevices of the vehicle, making his nose itch and his throat scratch. There was still no sign of any other car behind them, but he knew they were out there. Besides the worry about the men who were after them, there were plenty of other things to be concerned about— like running out of fuel or getting lost.

"It's getting worse," she said, staring out the window.

The howling winds seemed to cut right through the vehicle. A wall of sand rose up beside them. Issa took his foot off the gas, but it was too late. Darkness swept across the desert, blocking the light of the rising sun and turning visibility to zero in a matter of seconds.

"Hold on, everyone," Issa said.

Colton felt the tire on the driver's side hit something. The Jeep flipped once then somehow managed to land upright with one of the side windows shattered on impact. Sand swirled against his face like sharp needles. He turned to check on Lexi, but he couldn't open his eyes.

"Lexi... Bret?"

But the roar of the sand was all he could hear in response.

Lexi kept her eyes closed tight, praying for the sand and dust swirling through the car to settle. She couldn't move. Couldn't breathe. Her nose and throat felt as if she'd swallowed sandpaper. The temperature seemed to have risen in the past few seconds, adding to the discomfort of the suffocating conditions.

She listened for the others in the car, but all she could hear was the deafening sounds of the wind surrounding her. She managed to take off her seat belt, then pulled the scarf she'd been wearing around her neck and wrapped it around her face. But it wasn't enough to stop the sand from scraping against her face and neck.

She fought the panic. She'd heard of the blistering sandstorms that swept across the desert at the blink of an eye. And of men losing their way and dying from dehydration. She hoped that if she didn't move, she'd be okay. Issa and Colton would find a way out of this. All they had to do was wait for the storm to subside.

She remembered one of her coworkers was planning a romantic a trip into the desert on her next anniversary. Rennie had talked about the endless sand dunes, caravans of camels, camping among the Bedouin and watching the stars at night. No doubt there was beauty in the desert that she'd learned to appreciate, but not this way.

Then, as quickly as they had started, the violent winds began to calm.

She opened her eyes and saw Colton's solid form beside her.

She felt his hand against her arm. "Are you okay?"

She nodded, suddenly overwhelmed by emotion. The past two days had left her in a constant state of uncertainty.

"I've heard about sandstorms, but this…" She could barely describe it. The terror and fear that had swept in along with the wind.

"What about Bret and Issa…?" She let her voice trail off.

There was no movement from the front seat.

Colton grabbed her hand and helped her out of the vehicle. Bret's door was open, and there was no one in the front seat.

"This doesn't make sense," she said. "Why would they have left the vehicle?"

"I don't know."

She tried to shove away the looming panic. She wasn't sure how long they'd sat, waiting for the storm to pass. Five minutes? Ten? The two men had to be nearby. Neither would have risked moving out of the vehicle in the storm. And yet for some reason they had. She glanced out across waves of sand surrounding them. Now that the winds had died down the sun was shining just above the peaks of the dunes. She knew how confusing it had been when the storm had hit. And with Bret so weak, he could have woken up and panicked.

She turned back to Colton, feeling a sense of urgency grip her. They needed to get as far away from the men after them as possible and yet they couldn't leave without finding Bret and Issa. "What if Bret tried to escape the sandstorm? Issa must have realized it and went after him."

"It makes sense. He was groggy and confused." Colton jumped up on the hood of the car in order to see farther. "They still couldn't have gone far."

But there was no trace of Issa and Bret. And the wind had erased any footprints. She glanced back in the direction they'd come from. Neither were there signs of the men after them.

Colton jumped out of the car, then headed for the back of the vehicle, pausing beside a flat tire. "We definitely hit something back there."

Lexi felt a surge of adrenaline rush through her. If the other men were still behind them, they now had no way of escape.

"Should we try to go after Bret and Issa on foot?" Her heart was pounding. She needed something concrete to do.

Colton shook his head. "I'm afraid we'd get lost looking for them. If Issa's out there with Bret, he'll be okay."

"You don't know that." She shouted back at him, tired of constantly trying to prove she could handle everything that was going on. Tired of always trying to be okay. "We don't know that any of us are going to make it out of here alive."

Lexi pressed her lips together, regretting her sudden outburst. "I'm sorry."

"Don't be. You have nothing to apologize for." He walked back around the car to where she stood. "Nothing at all."

She bit her lip so she wouldn't cry. She was exhausted. Bret and Issa were missing. There were men out there looking for them. And now they were stranded in the middle of the Sahara with a flat tire on top of everything else.

Colton pressed his hands against her shoulders. "I've seen your strength, Lexi. Don't give up now. Issa knows this desert well, and is also extremely resourceful. And he would have been prepared for a situation like this. We need to make a quick inventory to see what we've got, and I need to change this tire, so that we can go as soon as they come back."

She nodded her head and took a deep breath. He was right. Panicking wasn't going to help.

"He's better prepared than I imagined," Colton said, opening up the back. "Besides the spare tire, there are several jugs of water, a shovel, a few jerry cans full of fuel, a first aid kit and a couple blankets."

"Okay. We've also got the backpack you brought with you from the plane." She grabbed it out of the backseat and started digging through it. "There are some water bottles, a first aid kit and a few power bars, along with yours and Bret's passports."

"At least we've got some food and water," Colton said, pulling out what he was going to need to change the tire. "What about the sat phone?"

"I think Issa had it with him in the front seat." She hurried back to the front of the car and pulled it out, then paused to look under that driver seat. Issa's handgun was gone.

"His gun isn't under the seat," she said.

"He must have taken it with him when he went to look for Bret."

Lexi heard the hesitation in Colton's voice. Something seemed off.

She looked down at the sat phone she was carrying. It still amazed her that Issa and his family could live in the middle of the Sahara and yet be so connected to the world. But she knew how important modern technology had proven to her. At times it had been her only link to the outside world. It gave her a chance not only keep in contact with the aid organization she worked for, but also with friends and family back in the States.

And gave Issa the ability to contact Salif or one of his men and strike a deal to trade Bret.

"How well do you know Issa?" she asked.

"What do you mean?"

"Is there a chance that he's not the friend you think he is?"

"Why would you say that? He's done nothing but protect us since he first found us after the crash."

"I know, but think about it. If he were to make a deal with Salif's men… All he'd have to do was hand over Bret for a percentage of the ransom. Ten…maybe twenty percent. That's a lot of money."

"No way." Colton shook his head.

"Just think about it, Colton. Issa and Bret disappear in the middle of a sandstorm. Issa's weapon is also gone. Something doesn't add up."

"He gave me a weapon, and there was no way he could have known about the storm or any of this. And if he wanted to turn us over to Salif's men, he could have done that back at the Kasbah, or even better when we ran into the men on the way to the Kasbah."

"I don't know. If they offered him more money… convinced him to help them. I don't want to be right, Colton, but none of this makes any sense." She glanced at the weapon next to him, knowing that any second now Salif's men could come into view and that they would barely have a fighting chance.

"I think you're wrong."

"Okay. Then tell me what we should do."

"Try to get my team on the sat phone while I change the tire. They need to be warned not to show up at the airstrip."

She sat down outside in the shade of the car and powered up the phone. Having something to do was the distraction she needed. The first time the connection failed. She tried again a second and third time, but again, both connections failed.

"Are you getting through?" Colton asked.

"No. So far I can't get a signal."

He continued to work on the tire, avoiding the obvious questions. Where were Issa and Bret? And where were the men who'd come after them at the Kasbah? It was clear that her words had upset him, but while he might not agree, she couldn't just dismiss the possibility.

Lexi brushed aside a loose strand of her hair from the corner of her mouth. "The battery is charged, so that's not the problem."

"I do know that the atmosphere can interfere with the reception from the satellite, and after the storm that just hit," he said, "honestly, I'd be more surprised if we did get through."

She worked on trying to get through for a couple of minutes.

"Tell me about the town you grew up in," he said, tugging on one of the lug nuts. "Big city or small town?"

Her brow rose at the question. She wanted to know

more about him. But not here. Over dinner at some nice restaurant, or at a picnic in a park.

"Small town on the coast of California. My grandparents owned a local five-and-dime store, then sold it to my parents when they retired."

She tried the connection again. If they didn't get through, his team most likely would walk into a trap.

"Wait… I think it's finally connecting."

He hurried over to her and she handed him the phone.

"This is Colton," he said putting it on Speaker.

"Colton… This is Jake. We were just getting ready to send someone after you."

"I need you to hold off on that."

"Hold off? I don't understand. I was told your plane went down."

"The men who took my brother-in-law…they're watching the airstrips. If you land, there's a good chance they'll be there waiting for you."

There was a short pause on the line. "But what about you and Bret?"

"We're going to try to get to Morocco and the embassy by car."

"That sounds risky. There's got to be another airstrip these guys aren't watching."

"But we have no way to know. They're already spread out across two countries."

"I still don't like the idea of leaving you on your own."

"I'm not sure how long the battery on this phone will last, so I'm going to need to keep it turned off, but we'll plan to check in every six hours."

There was nothing but static in reply.

"Can you hear me?" Colton asked.

Silence.

He let out a huff of air. "We lost the connection."

"Do you think he understood?"

"I hope so."

"Maybe meeting your team was worth the risk. They can't be at every airstrip across the desert."

"Before we do anything, we need to find Bret and Issa. I'm almost done changing the tire."

The sound of an engine roared behind them. Lexi turned around. Another 4x4 came over the ridge of a nearby sand dune headed right toward them.

"Any chance these are good guys out on a morning drive?" Lexi asked, taking a step backward.

He grabbed his gun off the top of the car "I'm not going to count on it."

She wanted to run, but there was nowhere to go.

Three men stepped out of their vehicle, guns pointed at her and Colton.

NINE

"Lexi…" Colton grabbed her arm and pushed her behind him in a desperate attempt to keep her from being injured, then disengaged his gun's safety and aimed the barrel at the men. He'd lost his brother-in-law somewhere out there in the desert. He wasn't going to let anything happen to Lexi, as well.

There were three men, dressed alike in fatigues and berets to block the sun. The tallest, took a step forward directing his own weapon back at Colton.

"If you hadn't noticed there are three of us, each with a loaded weapon, and only two of you and one weapon," he said in a thick accent. "So I'd advise you to not even attempt to play hero."

The man was clearly the leader, but the other two had the same look of arrogance in their eyes. They were in control and they knew it.

"What do you want?" Colton asked.

"We've have orders to bring you to see Salif. He's not happy about what happened at the camp yesterday."

Losing out on both two million dollars and a number of his men had to have been quite a blow to Salif. But nothing was going to change this time. Even if they kidnapped the two of them, coming up with two million dollars wasn't going to happen. And he had the feeling Lexi's brother wasn't going to be able to resolve the situation either, even if they did found him.

"And if we'd rather stay here?" Colton asked.

"This isn't a negotiation. It's an order."

Colton hesitated as he tried to weigh his options. But at the moment they didn't have any. They were outnumbered and outgunned. And if Lexi's theory was correct, then Issa wasn't going to show up and rescue them.

Unless Issa really was the friend he believed him to be.

Colton stared out at the rolling desert beyond the men. Issa was the only backup they had at the moment. Which meant there was only one way out of this. He needed to stall and pray that Issa showed up.

"Where are you planning to take us?" he asked, squeezing Lexi's fingers gently with his free hand.

"Salif's waiting at his compound. He didn't take kindly to the ambush on his men."

"You give them too much information, Hamid. We need to leave."

Hamid laughed. "It's not as if they're going anywhere."

Colton frowned. He'd been told by the army that they were dealing with a small group of "work-for-hire fighters." Which meant that not only had the army's assessment of who they were dealing with been way off, they had also failed to carry out their job in taking down the group of insurgents. There had been no win-win situation. And they were now on their own.

Where are you, Issa?

He had to keep stalling.

"How much does Salif pay you to do his dirty work?" Colton asked.

"His dirty work?" The shorter of the men kicked at the sand in front of him. "What business is that of yours?"

"The military is underpaid," Colton continued, "so I'm assuming you make more than they do. And the average worker's annual salary in this country is fifteen hundred American dollars a year, which is enough to scrape by. So I'm curious. Two million dollars goes a long way, but I have a feeling most of that doesn't go into your pockets."

The men stared at him.

"How many kidnappings has Salif been involved in this year? Five? Ten? When those families pay, that would be what…a minimum of ten million dollars? And yet it's likely that none of you ever see that money."

"That is not your business." Hamid took a step forward, the tension in his jaw evident. "Though he might pay us extra to shoot both of you, which I'd be happy to do if you don't shut up."

Colton ignored the threat as he scanned the desert for any sign of Issa. He wasn't going to be able to stall much longer. But Lexi couldn't be right. Issa wouldn't betray him. Not for money. His team had saved both Issa's wife and his son, and since then, they'd continued rely on Issa to be a bridge between the mission organization and the villages scattered across the region.

But if he was wrong…

"Enough talk." The leader took a step forward, his gun steady. "Put your weapon down, or I'll shoot the girl."

Colton hesitated for another couple seconds, then laid the gun on the sand in front of him.

Show me what to do, God.

The men nodded for them to walk toward their Land Rover. There would be no more stalling. He grabbed Lexi's hand to ensure she stayed right beside him.

After two months of captivity, Bret hadn't been killed by the insurgents. Which meant their hostages were worth more alive than dead. But how long could he and Lexi expect to keep their lives when the US wouldn't pay the ransom? Their families couldn't pay the ransom. There was a possibility that his mission organization would try to raise the funds, but that money wasn't going to be easy to come up with.

Colton stopped his progress toward the vehicle. There were still no signs of Issa and Bret, but they had to be out there. Waiting for an opportunity.

"Let me just ask you one more question before we leave," he said.

Hamid stepped up to Colton. Close enough that he could smell the other man's foul breath. "What are you doing? Waiting for your guide to show up and rescue you again? Because it's not going to happen."

Colton felt a wave of anger surge inside his gut. "What did you do with him?"

"Colton, don't—"

But Lexi's warning came too late. Colton felt the butt of the gun smash against his head. And then nothing.

Colton felt a stab of pain shoot across the side of his head. He forced himself to open his eyes, then tried focusing on a sliver of light in the darkness. He was lying down. Temples throbbing. Jaw tight. Small snippets of memories slowly began to surface. Someone had been chasing them. Their car had flipped. Bret and Issa had vanished. Salif's men had shown up. And Lexi—

Spots dotted his vision. His chest tightened as a wave of dizziness swept over him. Where was Lexi?

"Colton?"

He shifted his head at the sound of her voice, this time ignoring the throbbing pain. Relief swept through him as he found her sitting cross-legged beside him.

"How are you feeling?" she asked.

He glanced around the dark space. He was lying on a mat inside a tent. He had no idea where, but at least they were together. "I feel like I've been hit over the head with a brick."

"Try the butt of a riffle." Her voice was soft. On edge. "You were out the whole way here. I've been worried."

"I'll live." He pressed his hand against his temple and discovered the painful lump. "You didn't happen to grab that backpack, did you?"

"I did actually," she said, pulling out the water and a couple of painkillers. "They took the knife, but surprisingly let us keep the rest."

"My throbbing head is forever grateful," he said, downing the pills. "What about you? Are you okay? Or at least as okay as possible after being kidnapped by a bunch of insurgents for the second time in two days."

She shot him a half smile, but it quickly faded. "I'm scared. I don't see a way out this time, and I'm pretty sure you have a mild concussion."

"But they want us alive, remember. At least that's

still in our favor." He glanced at the streak of light coming through the tent flap. "So where exactly are we?"

"As promised, they brought us to their compound to see Salif."

"How long have we been here?"

"Not long."

He caught the fear in her eyes and felt a twinge of regret over his decision. He'd pushed the men too hard and in turn had put her life in danger. And yet what else could he have done? If Issa had been out there…

But Hamid had been right. Issa wasn't coming to his rescue. Not this time.

"I was trying to stall them," he said, catching her gaze. "I was counting on Issa to show up. Three against two didn't seem like bad odds, but this…"

"I know and I'm sorry," she whispered.

So was he. What was Becca going to do when they didn't show up in Morocco? Or if she received another ransom call?

I don't know what to do, God. You called me here to protect and serve, but I'm out of options.

He glanced at Lexi. There was something reassuring about her presence. But he also knew how scared she was. He needed to find a way to end this.

"Do you still believe Issa's in on this?" he asked.

"I don't know."

"Have you seen him?"

Lexi shook her head.

"They had to have been out there somewhere."

"What do we do now?" she asked. "If I can't find Trent, they won't need me anymore. And even if I did know where he was, no matter what he's done, I don't know… I don't know if I can betray him."

* * *

Lexi watched Colton in the dimly lit space. Frustration over her brother's behavior—and the subsequent consequences—had continued to trouble her. She had no idea where he was. No idea what exactly he'd done. All she knew for sure was that the nightmare had begun again. Another makeshift compound with nothing more than a few tents and a cooking hut all surrounded by the vast desert.

Sweat beaded across her neck and ran down her back in the sweltering heat. But no matter how angry she might feel, her brother's actions were the least of her worries right now. Colton needed medical attention, especially if he had a concussion. And on top of that, they had to find out what had happened to Bret and Issa.

She had no way to contact Colton's mission, and even if they did, what could they do? If the army had been unable to take out the insurgents, a group of aid workers certainly weren't going to be able to.

"We have to find a way out of here," she said, keeping her voice at a whisper.

"I agree," he said, "but the last time I had the aid of the army and that didn't exactly end the way I'd planned."

Colton shifted on the mat. She knew what he was thinking. Salif's men had weapons capable of taking down his Cessna. How in the world were they supposed to fight against them?

He turned onto his side and started to push himself up.

"Colton?" She reached out to steady him. "You're not fine."

"I'm just a little dizzy."

She frowned. "Lie back down, then. You need to rest."

He waived her off, then pressed his hands against the sides of the mat for balance. "I'm okay, and you're right. We need an escape strategy to get out of here. Can you guess at how many men are in the camp?"

She caught the determination in his eyes along with the bruise that was forming on his forehead. She couldn't help wonder what plan they could come up with that would actually work. But if nothing else, this would help make her feel more in control.

"They brought us straight from the Land Rover to here," she said. "The camp is small, and I saw about a dozen men. Most of them were carrying AK-4/s."

"What about vehicles and other weapons?"

"I saw three vehicles including the one they brought us here in. And as for weapons? Like I said most of the men are armed, but there's no way to know what might be inside in the other tents."

"Okay…" He pressed his hand against the back of his neck, clearly in pain. "I'm assuming they move around frequently, in order to avoid detection, so they would want to travel light when they do. Salif might have a permanent base somewhere, but if he knows the government is looking for him, lying low for a while would make sense."

"Somehow I don't think they're going to offer us a tour."

Colton let out a low chuckle. "Unfortunately I think you're right."

She heard two men arguing outside, their voices getting louder as they approached the tent.

"Someone's coming," she whispered, grasping Colton's forearm.

They hadn't spoken to anyone since they'd arrived, but she knew that eventually Salif was going to want to talk to them and tell them exactly what he wanted. A shadow crossed in front of the flap of their tent. At the same time she heard someone call out. It must have been to the men who were approaching because their voices faded in the afternoon air and the shadow receded as they walked away.

"So do you think our best way out of here is one of the vehicles?" she asked, letting out a breath of relief at the delay.

"It's risky, but it seems like that's our only option. The only problem is even if we did manage to steal one of the vehicles, then what? We don't have any idea where we are."

Lexi bit the edge of her lip. He was right. They had no maps, and barely any supplies. Even if they did make it out, where were they going to go? They were miles away from the nearest town.

"You know what I want right now?" Colton asked.

Her eyes narrowed as she caught his gaze. "What?"

"Becca makes this s'mores cheesecake. It's this amazing dessert with layers of chocolate and marshmallows and hot fudge sauce. It's sickeningly sweet and absolutely delicious."

Lexi chuckled at his craving. "I'm hungry, but even that's sounds way too sweet to me. Personally, I'd settle for some lemonade with ice and one of my dad's burgers straight off the grill. I haven't had a decent hamburger for months."

"I wouldn't mind that with a side order of onion rings and a thick chocolate shake—"

"Stop." She scooted over a few inches in order to lean back against the wooden pole holding up the center of the tent. "What made you think of your sister's dessert?"

"Besides the fact that I'm hungry?" He shook his head. "I keep thinking about Becca and what she's going to do when I don't call her."

She could hear the frustration in his voice.

"My stepfather's expecting me to come home and now…I don't know what's going to happen."

Or when he was going to hear from her.

A stab of pain shot through her. Her stepfather had already lost her mother. Which was why her decision to leave the US and work in Africa had already come at a cost to her family. They'd understood, or at least had tried to understand, but she knew they worried about her living in an unstable region no matter how many precautions she'd promised them she was taking.

Colton reached out and brushed his fingers against the back of her hand. "I'm so sorry you're having to go through all of this again."

His touch sent shivers through her. In another place and time, she could see herself falling for someone like him. She'd seen firsthand his integrity. His willingness to risk his life for others. His strength. She pushed away any thoughts of romance. All she needed to be thinking about right now was surviving. And finding a way out of here.

"Lexi?"

"I'm okay. It's just hard not to wonder if we're ever going to see our families. Or if we're going to have the chance to do something…normal. I'd do anything for a boring trip to the grocery store. But what about your head?" she said, changing the subject. "Any better yet?"

"The pain's a bit less."

The shadow of a man appeared in the open flap of the tent again, blocking their only source of light. Hamid, one of the men who'd grabbed them earlier, stepped inside, then ordered her to come with him.

Colton reached for her hand and squeezed her fingers. "Lexi—"

"I'll be fine."

She swallowed hard, hoping her words sounded more confident than she felt. But Colton was right—they needed her alive.

Outside the tent, she walked across the hot sand ahead of the insurgent who held his AK-57 pointed at her back. Not that he needed it…she wasn't going anywhere. The heat of the late morning sun beat across her head and shoulders. Forget an ice-cold lemonade. She'd be happy with anything wet to drink at this point.

Wiping the sweat off back of her neck, Lexi drew in a deep breath and took in as many details around her as she could. Four men lounged in the shade of one of the tents. Another four stood around the perimeter guarding the camp against any threat that might arise behind the waves of sand in the distance. To her right there was a narrow row of solar panels—an attempt to modernize the compound—and beyond them, she noted that one of the vehicles was gone from where it had been parked when they'd arrived. She'd heard an engine running before Colton had woken up, and couldn't help but wonder where it had gone. There was still no sign of Issa or Bret. Would they have taken the men to another camp?

They stopped in front of a bearded man sitting on a wooden chair and eating an almost-empty plate of stew and bread.

"You and your friend have caused me a lot of grief," he said, not stopping to look at her as he sopped up the last bite of stew with the bread. "But I learned a long time ago that things don't always go as planned."

"You must be Salif," she said, trying not to sound as if she was about to pass out.

"I believe the last time you were in my custody, my men asked you where your brother was. I'm asking you again." He dropped the empty plate onto the ground next to him and looked up at her. "And this time I want an answer."

Help me know what I should say, God. Please...

Lexi drew in a slow breath as she fought the panic threatening to overwhelm her. "And I told them what I knew. He came to visit me and then he left. He didn't tell me where he was going, and I haven't heard from him since."

"So I've been told. But surely you have some idea where he might be, because helping me is by far your better option."

She reached up unconsciously and felt the place where Amar had slapped her face. They believed she was hiding something, that she knew where her brother was. It was probably the only reason she was alive. But what would happen when they realized she was telling the truth and had no idea where Trent was or where to find him? Then what?

"What do you want me to do?" she asked.

"We're going to send him a video. He won't reply to me or my messages, but perhaps he will respond to his sister if he knows her life is on the line."

She caught the man's gaze and saw the spite in his eyes. He was telling the truth. She had to get through to Trent. Because as soon as she lost her value to them, they would kill her.

TEN

Lexi tried to swallow the fear, not wanting Salif to know how terrified she really was. She knew enough about the man to understand that he had little to lose and everything to gain. But that didn't mean he was going to win. Not this time. There had to be a way to find Bret, get them out of here and put an end to this.

Salif spoke to Hamid, who immediately went running to a nearby tent. "He'll be back in a minute with a video camera. And while he's gone, you can think about what you're going to say. All you have to do is convince your brother this isn't a game."

Lexi frowned at the implications, still trying to win the battle against her growing nerves.

"Tell me exactly what Trent did," she said, turning back to Salif while they waited for the other man to return. She was going to need answers if she ever expected to wrap her mind around the situation.

"I assumed you knew."

"I don't think he wanted me to know. He told me he was coming to visit me. That it was a long-overdue vacation. He never told me he was in trouble."

"Then let's just say he's made a few people very angry."

"Including yourself?"

"I'm more of a middleman. I do the occasional work-for-hire. Your brother has been embezzling money from a business partner who I happen to know quite well.

Salif wiped his mouth with the back of his hand. "I'm here to ensure my friend gets his money back."

"And he doesn't care who is hurt in the meantime?" Her voice broke, but she wasn't finished. "Or if someone dies in the process?"

"Your brother made a number of foolish decisions, which means he is the one who will have to live with any consequences."

And Trent had to have known about those consequences. He realized he was about to get caught and knew if he didn't run, he'd end up in prison or more likely, dead. So he'd decided to disappear to Africa. And in the process, he'd managed to drag her into the situation.

"And what do you get for tracking him down?" Lexi asked.

"A nice paycheck. And a sign of goodwill."

"And Trent? What happens to him if you find him?"

"Why would you care?" Salif said. "Sounds to me as if he betrayed you."

"He's family," she said, wondering if there was anything she could say that would change his mind. "My mother died a few months ago, and my father—"

"Forget the sob story. It won't work." Salif let out a deep chuckle.

Apparently she'd been wrong to think she might find a layer of humanity beneath his gruff exterior.

"Once he is found, he will be dealt with appropriately. But he chose the wrong place to run. He apparently had no idea that the man he swindled has contacts all across North Africa." His smile quickly faded. "And here's another problem. This entire situation has become personal. Besides the two-million-dollar ransom, I also lost some of my best men in that raid by the army. I can't simply just pretend that didn't happen."

"I had nothing to do with any of that."

"That doesn't really matter. I have a feeling Colton's family will be a bit more forthcoming with the money this time when they realize this isn't a game."

"Then what do you want me to do?"

"We're going to make sure your brother realizes that he will need to come forward and replace the money he stole...or you will die."

Or you will die.

Lexi replayed the words in her mind as Hamid returned with the video camera and handed it to Salif.

"You might be surprised how high-tech we manage to be out here in the middle of nowhere. I can create a video with a sat phone and on the internet I can send it anywhere in the world I want."

Hamid secured Lexi's hands behind her back, then shoved her onto the chair where Salif had been eating minutes ago. She winced as her arm scraped against the rough wood. This was not idle conversation. He didn't care what happened to her. Because for him, this was nothing more than a business deal, and she had become a disposable commodity.

Thirty seconds later, Hamid was running the video while Salif stood next to her, making his demands into the camera, and then turned to Lexi.

"Tell your brother what I said."

Lexi swallowed hard. "Trent…listen to him. You have forty-eight hours. And if you don't show up… they will kill me."

Salif motioned for Hamid to turn off the video. Speaking the words again out loud spread a wave of nausea through her.

"Take her back to her tent," Salif said, "Then we'll send this to a place Trent will be sure and see it."

But Lexi knew the truth. Just because Trent saw the video didn't mean he'd respond, or that she was going to be enough motivation to return the money he'd embezzled. Not that he'd ever want her dead, but he'd chosen to run and more than likely didn't have access to pay back what he'd stolen. Which meant they had less than forty-eight hours to find a way out of here.

Hamid unbound her, but kept a firm grip on her arm. Lexi winced at the irony. He might be setting her free, but they knew, as well as she did, that there was no way out of here.

"What about Issa and Bret?" she said to Salif before turning away. "Do you have them, too?"

"They told me you were trying to stall when my men picked you up. I'm going to assume you were waiting for Issa to come to your rescue again." Salif rested his hands against his hips. "But he's not coming. Not this time. I can promise you that."

"Then where is he?"

Salif nodded at Hamid without answering her question.

Hamid tightened the grip on her arm and forced her back to the tent. Colton was pacing inside the small

space. She waited a few seconds for her eyes to adjust
to the dimness.

"Lexi?"

"I'm okay. I just… I need to sit down." Her legs felt
as if they were about to give out on her. The surge of
adrenaline had started to wear off, leaving her feeling
as if she were about to crash. In all the training she
gone through before she came, none of it had prepared
her for this. She was tired and overwhelmed. She sat
down on the mat and took in a deep breath.

*I don't know how much more of this I can handle,
God. I feel as if I've been pushed to my limits…*

"They didn't hurt you—"

"No. But it's like this is all a game to him, and I'm
simply a stepping-stone to getting what he wants."

She'd looked into Salif's eyes and had left wondering if there was any sense of humanity in him. Instead
she saw a cycle of greed. Her brother's greed. Salif's
greed…

Colton sat down across from her. A ray of light coming in from the flap of the tent cast a shadow across
Colton's face. His face was pale and the spot where
they'd struck him on his temple was now turning a
deep shade of purple. But he hadn't lost that fierce
determination in his eyes. Part of her wanted to curl
up in a ball in his arms and sleep until this was over.
But that kind of escape wasn't going to help them find
a way out.

"What did they want?" he asked.

"They made a video with their demands to Trent."

"And their demands?"

She picked at a hole in the mat, not wanting to tell
him everything. There was nothing he could do to

change things. Plans of escape might keep them busy, but the reality was that their options were limited.

Colton frowned when she didn't answer. "What else did they say?"

She flicked at a broken nail. Funny how six months ago, she never missed a manicure. Somehow all of that didn't matter anymore.

"My brother embezzled a large amount of money from a man he was working for," she said.

"And…"

"They gave him forty-eight hours to come forward, or they will kill me."

"They're bluffing, Lexi—"

"I don't think so. They've shown they have patience, but they also they shot our plane down. Hunted us down at the Kasbah. And now they've taken us. These men won't think twice about killing someone if it means getting what they want. That's what they do." There was no inflection in her voice as she caught his gaze. "And it might end up costing both of us our lives."

Colton massaged the back of his neck with his fingers, but it did little to relieve the growing tension. "You're not responsible for your brother's actions."

He paused at the irony of his words. How many times had his mother thrown that same line at him when it came to his father? He might not have been responsible for his father's actions, but that hadn't kept him from having to deal with the consequences.

Just like Lexi was having to deal with the ramifications of her brother's choices.

"You're wrong. This is my fault." Tears welled in her eyes as she looked up at him. "I should have figured out what he was up to when he was staying with me. Instead, I wanted to think that he'd grown up. That things had changed between us and for whatever reason he wanted to come see me. But I should have known. He was simply using me."

"Stop." He ran his hand down her arm until his fingers caught her hand. "I meant what I said. This wasn't your fault."

She shrugged. "Maybe you're right, but even if you are, it doesn't matter. We're still here, and I don't see any way of that changing."

"Lexi—"

"When I arrived, I thought I was strong enough to handle whatever I had to do. I've seen so much heartache over the past few months, and yet that very heartache is what kept me going. Every day, I watch women and children spend hours collecting water. I met mothers who lost their babies because they didn't have access to a clean water supply. Health care facilities and schools lack adequate sanitation. I thought that if I could just change things for a handful of people my contribution would matter."

"It does matter."

"But today…" She looked up at him. "I don't feel strong anymore. I don't know how to handle this."

She was crying silently now, the tears evident on her cheeks. "I'm scared, Colton. We'll never get out of here with one of the vehicles. There are too many guards. Too many weapons."

Colton pulled her against his chest, knowing that every answer he could think of seemed trite. He didn't know if everything was going to work out. Didn't know if they would walk away from this alive. And no matter how badly he wanted to, he couldn't promise her any of those things.

She lay still until her breathing became steadier. She felt comfortable against him. A perfect fit. He tried to ignore the thought as he pushed back a strand of her hair and looped it behind her ear. There was something about her, though, that had managed to weave its way into his heart when he wasn't looking. Something that made him wonder again if an ongoing relationship might be a possibility once they were out of here.

"Thank you," she said, looking up at him.

"For what?"

"For not promising me that everything's going to be okay. For just listening and being there for me."

He nodded, wishing he could give her more. "You're welcome."

She wiped her cheeks, then sat back, though still close enough that their knees were barely touching. "I'm the kind of person who needs to have a plan."

"Okay."

"I need to figure out where my brother might have gone."

"Who did your brother work for back in the States?" he asked.

"Honestly, I'm not sure."

"Okay, then just tell me what you do know about him."

"He's twenty-six. Knows he's charming and knows how to make people laugh. He's never held down a job for long, floats from one place to another, looking for the next payoff. He's suave and a bit of a con. Has always got by on his good looks."

"You said the two of you weren't close."

"Not really."

"What about your stepfather and their relationship? Would he go back home?"

"He might. My stepfather spoiled him growing up. That's probably part of why he's not responsible. He always used to bail him out. Though when he came to see me he paid for his own ticket."

"Did he go out at night?"

"Yeah. He made friends with a few ex-pats and met them for drinks a few times."

"Any strange conversations you overheard, or anything that seems off now that you're looking back?"

"I heard him talking on the phone one evening. I didn't really think much about it at the time, but he seemed... I don't know. Upset. Like he was afraid something he was working on was about to fall through. But while I knew he had a few questionable friends, I never thought he could be this stupid."

"Do you think he wanted to tell you the truth?"

She pondered his question for a minute. "Looking back, I think he didn't know what to do and had no idea what the consequences were going to be. He's not a horrible person. Just in way over his head."

"What about his airline ticket? Where had he planned to go when he left you?"

"He was planning to fly to Morocco."

"Did he know anyone there?" Colton asked.

"I don't know. He didn't tell me much about his plans."

The bottom line was that Trent was going to have to come forward on his own. But he wasn't sure her brother was man enough to do so.

He shot her a reassuring smile, hoping to convince

her that this wasn't a hopeless situation. "You said Salif mentioned he had a sat phone."

"Yeah."

"If we could somehow get a hold of it, it's possible for someone on the outside to track the phone through the built-in GPS."

"Even if we were able to manage that, who would we call?"

Colton knew that with the growing number of terrorist organizations that threatened American interests, there were special operations located throughout North Africa.

"I have no idea how many special operations bases there are, but I do know that the US has a footprint all over Africa, including the Sahara. And while our government might not pay ransom, there are military resources who might be able to help."

Lexi frowned. "They didn't help with Bret."

"We didn't know where he was until I made the swap."

But could he really expect the US troops to sweep in and snatch them from the middle of the Sahara?

"Do you really think it's worth the risk?" she asked. "Trying to get the phone?"

"I think we need to keep our eyes open for an opportunity."

"I asked about Issa and Bret."

"And?"

"He wouldn't answer me as to where they were. But he did promise me Issa wasn't going to rescue us this time."

"Do you think they're here?"

"I don't know, but I *do* think they have them. It's

the only thing that makes sense. They have the man-
power and the weapons to conduct a search. Even if it
is in the middle of the desert."

"What about me?"

"Salif didn't say anything about you."

It was strange they hadn't brought him to talk with
Salif. Was Becca's life truly in danger? Or were they
waiting to find Bret so they would have more leverage?

The dreams were back. He was running again. This
time through an endless brick maze, with faceless men
behind him. They were gaining on him. For every step
he took, they came closer until they were breathing
down his neck.

Colton opened his eyes where he lay on the hard
mat and stared up. His heart pounding as if he had
actually been running. In the faint light, he could see
Lexi on the other side of the tent. He wasn't sure if she
was sleeping, but if she was, he didn't want to wake
her. She needed her rest. They both did. And they also
needed a plan.

He'd heard the fear in her voice. She believed without a doubt that Salif would follow through with his
threats. And he had to admit she was probably right.

He drew in a deep breath, trying to slow down his
breathing. No matter what they did, it seemed like a
no-win situation.

So what were they supposed to do? They'd have as
much of a chance of delivering the moon as they would
have coming up with the two million dollars. And who
knew where Lexi's brother was, or if they found him,
if there was any money left to repay the partner he'd
embezzled from.

So what happens now, God?

Becca and Noah were in hiding. He had no way to communicate with anyone for help. They could make a run for it and pray they didn't get shot in the process. He wasn't sure he believed Issa and Bret had been captured, but if they had, would he and Lexi be sealing their fates if they ran?

"Colton?"

He turned back over, the sudden movement shooting pain through his head. It took him a moment for his eyes to adjust.

"Lexi?"

"No, it's Issa."

"Issa?"

"Don't talk right now, but I need you to get up. I'm going to get you and Lexi out of here."

Colton had to still be dreaming.

Issa couldn't be here. Or maybe it was a trap.

"Colton? We don't have time to wait. I need you to come with me now."

ELEVEN

Lexi stepped out of the tent behind Colton and Issa into almost total darkness. The moon was temporarily hidden behind a row of clouds and the only light was coming from a few stars overhead. But it wouldn't stay hidden for long. She could feel the breeze and see the break in the clouds above her. If they were going to do this without being seen, they were going to have to hurry.

Colton took her hand as they darted behind the tent. She had a dozen questions for Issa, but knew she was going to have to wait until they were away from the compound before she got any answers. And for the moment, they were going to have to trust him. Because every second it took them to escape was another chance to be discovered.

A shadow shifted to their left. One of the guards was making his way toward them. She glanced at Issa. He had his weapon, but they would be no match against the dozen armed men in the camp if they were caught trying to escape.

Issa held up his hand, motioning for them to pull back into a small alcove between the tents. Lexi drew in a lungful of air and held her breath. Footsteps came toward them. She glanced up at the sky. The moon was beginning to slip out from behind the blanket of clouds. In another few seconds its white light would cover the camp, leaving them vulnerable if they didn't cross over the ridge behind them and disappear from sight.

Lexi pressed against Colton's chest and let him wrap his arms around her as they waited for the man to pass. She could feel Colton's heart beating. Feel his chest expanding with each breath…

The guard paused a dozen feet from where they stood. Close enough for her to see the silhouette of his weapon across his shoulder and the glint of a knife in his belt. She couldn't move. Colton's arm tightened around her waist. All the guard had to do was turn around and he'd see them…

But he only hesitated a moment longer, then kept moving in the other direction.

Lexi let out a sharp sigh of relief as he faded into the darkness. "There are three other guards patrolling,"

"Then we need to move now," Issa whispered. He started toward the open desert, in the opposite direction of the camp, as another cloud rolled by, concealing the moon once again.

Lexi's lungs threatened to burst as she ran beside Colton up a slight ridge of sand. She glanced back, expecting to see someone coming after them. She'd been this close to freedom before only to discover it was nothing more than a mirage and she'd been forced to go through it all over again. But this time…

Please, God. Let this be over.

Because if they came after them now… She'd seen Salif's eyes. He would kill them.

Issa topped the ridge, then scurried down the other side of the sand dune before pausing to let them catch their breath. "I don't see any signs that we were followed, but we must leave quickly."

"Where's Bret?" Colton asked.

"Just over the next ridge," Issa said, jutting his chin away from the camp. "I couldn't drive the vehicle close to the camp, and we decided he wasn't strong enough to make the trek here and back. So I came alone."

"But he's okay." Colton asked.

"He's going to be fine. He's just weak." Issa started walking again. "Can you both make it? The Jeep's about half a kilometer out."

"Yeah. Of course," Colton said. "Lexi?"

Her heart was still pounding and the adrenaline had yet to stop flowing, but she was okay. "I'll be fine."

"Salif implied that his men had found you and Bret," Colton said, as they hurried across the sand.

"Then that was what he wanted you to believe. We saw them searching for us several times, but managed to evade them."

"I still don't understand where you went," Colton said, asking one of the questions she wanted answered.

Issa paused and caught Colton's gaze. Even in the darkness she could see the confusion in his eyes. "You thought I betrayed you?"

"I honestly didn't know what to think. I know you have always been a faithful friend, but when the two of you disappeared…"

"Do not blame yourself," Issa said, walking again. "I took my gun, and left the car with your brother-in-law. If I run the scenario through my mind, I might have come to the same conclusions as you did. There are men who would betray another for a lesser price."

"So what did happen?" Lexi asked, hurrying to keep up with the men.

"During the sandstorm—after the wreck—Bret woke up and was confused. The car was filled with sand and the sounds of the storm. When I realized he was getting out of the car, there was nothing I could do but go after him, knowing how quickly he could get lost out there.

"I grabbed my weapon for safety, knowing you had one as well if you needed it, and went after him. I didn't expect him to go far, but adrenaline must have been working with the storm, and I struggled to keep up with him. He finally collapsed about a kilometer from the vehicle. By the time I finally managed to get him to come back with me and to tell you what was going on, they were leading you to their car. But I was afraid to risk leaving Bret alone and come to help you, because if I had gotten caught—"

"You would have left Bret exposed in the middle of the desert, and he could have died," Colton finished for him.

A wave of guilt flooded through Lexi. She never should have doubted the man's innocence. Since he and his caravan first came upon them at the wreckage site, he'd done everything he could to protect them.

"Issa… I'm sorry," she said.

He shook his head. "You have nothing to be sorry for."

"I was the one who doubted your loyalty. Not Colton. You've done nothing but help us, and now you have risked your life to come back for us. You didn't have to do this."

He paused beneath the ribbon of stars shining above them. "But you are wrong. Colton and his team saved my son's and my wife's lives. I would do anything to repay that debt."

"There is no debt," Colton said, gripping the man's shoulder. "Only friendship."

The shadow of the Jeep appeared as they topped another ridge of sand.

"Here we are," Issa said, as they hurried down the mound. "Thankfully, they left the vehicle fairly intact after only stealing some of my supplies. The wind had completely died down, so after I finished changing the tire, I was able to follow the tire tracks to the camp."

Bret was sitting in the front passenger seat with the door open. He still seemed a bit pale, but looked far better than the last time she'd seen him.

Colton leaned inside the car and grabbed his brother-in-law in a bear hug. "Bret! You don't know how happy I am to see you. How are you feeling?"

"Honestly, I haven't felt this good in weeks. Partly because the pain from the scorpion bite is gone, but mainly because I'm closer to being back with my family again."

"We're going to get you home," Colton said, squeezing Bret's shoulder.

"I hate to break up the happy reunion," Issa said, "but we must hurry. I have a feeling it won't take them long to discover you are gone. And once they do…"

Lexi glanced at Colton. Issa didn't need to finish his sentence. The men from the camp would come after them, which meant they needed to put as much distance between themselves and the camp as possible.

"So what do we do now?" Lexi asked as she climbed into the backseat of the vehicle beside Colton.

"We need to make it to the Moroccan border," Issa said. "I'm hoping the three of you will be safe there, and it will be easy to catch a flight out of North Africa."

Lexi felt her stomach churn. Crossing the border wouldn't be easy under the best circumstance, but unlike Colton and Bret, she didn't even have her passport. And they'd never be able to smuggle a passenger across the border, where armed guards patrolled day and night. These uniformed men had the right to search any vehicle and were not above using intimidation and demanding bribes.

We've come this far, God, but I don't see how this is going to work.

How was she supposed to leave the country without proper documentation?

"I don't have a passport," she said above the rumbling of the vehicle. "They'll never let me through."

"She is right," Issa said. "Not without paying a bribe or managing to convince someone of your story and the need to get to your embassy."

Colton reached out and squeezed her hand "We're going to get you home. We'll find a way. I promise."

She nodded, hoping he was right, but the sick feeling in her stomach refused to dissipate.

An hour later, Colton glanced out the back window. A puff of dust hovered on the horizon behind them, a sign that someone was following them. Again, he weighed his options, but they were driving across open desert. The track Issa was following in his 4x4 was eroded and more often than not obscured by dirt and sand, but it was the only route to the border.

And that wasn't the only issue they faced. He'd caught the worry in Lexi's voice when they'd discussed the border crossing. He hoped he sounded more convincing than he felt. Walking across the border without a passport wasn't an option. If discovered, they'd arrest her, unless they offered the authorities a bribe. He had a little cash that might buy her way across, but was it going to be enough? It was going to depend on who was there, and what kind of day they were having.

He blew out a sharp huff of air. There was nothing they could do about it at this point. With Morocco their quickest way out of Africa, they were going to need to take their chances.

"They're behind us, aren't they?" Lexi asked, breaking the long silence.

"Someone's back there," Colton said.

He'd caught Issa looking out the rearview mirror every few minutes, but hadn't said anything. So far, it didn't seem like their pursuers were gaining on them, but how long could Issa maintain his distance from vehicle. And what was going to happen once they got to the border?

Lexi glanced out the back window. "I don't understand how they keep finding us."

"It's not necessarily Salif's men," Bret said.

"True, but neither can we assume it's simply a group of tourists," Issa said, his hands tightly gripping the steering wheel as they flew across the desert. "Salif has proven to have far more resources than I expected."

"And you're sure we're going in the right direction?" Lexi asked. "It just feels as if we're going in circles."

He'd felt the same thing. The terrain had become an endless monotony of sand and scrub bushes. The hot sun simmered above them in a cloudless sky. There were no visible landmarks. Nothing distinguishing their route beyond the faint tracks they followed.

"My father taught me to read the desert like you read a map. At night we followed the stars. In the daylight, I learned every tree, every ruin and every shadow. This after years of driving across this desert from Timbuktu to Nouadhibou."

"What did your father do?"

Issa chuckled. "That is a question better left unasked."

"How close are they?" Bret asked.

"It's hard to tell." Colton glanced behind him again at the flat expanse. "At least a kilometer. Maybe a bit more."

"We're going to need to stop," Issa said. "The fuel tank's almost on empty, and I need to check the water. The terrain is brutal on the vehicles and this one tends to overheat, which we can't allow to happen. Thankfully the men missed one of the jerry cans of fuel under the backseat."

Issa glanced at Colton. "I'm going to need you to stand guard."

Colton glanced behind him.

"What can I do?" Bret asked.

"I've got a second weapon," Issa said. "A small handgun."

"Then let me have it. If nothing else, I can fire a

gun. You might not remember, Colton, but my aim's pretty good."

He knew Bret had military training, but still… "You're in no condition to—"

"We're going to need all the help we can get," Issa said, interrupting Colton. He nodded, hating the fact that Issa was right. But if they ended up having to face off with Salif's men, they were going to need Bret.

"And I can check the fluid levels," Lexi offered.

"Okay," Colton said. "Then I'm guessing we've got about one minute. A minute and a half at the most."

"Agreed," Issa said. "And we won't be able to stop again until we get to the border."

Colton grabbed the weapon sitting beside Issa, his body pumping with adrenaline. They had to do this, but every second they were parked, meant a second gained on them by the car following them.

He turned to Lexi. "You okay?"

She glanced at the weapon he was holding. "Not really."

He reached out and squeezed her hand. "Just keep praying. We can do this."

He could see the fear in her eyes as she nodded, but he also didn't miss the determination.

I don't know how this is going to end, God, but protect her, please. Protect all of us.

"Everyone ready?" Issa asked.

The vehicle ground to a stop, and the four of them jumped out. Lexi popped the hood while Issa grabbed the jerry can and started filling the tank. Colton and Bret flanked the back of the car, ready to stop whoever was coming toward them.

Fifteen seconds passed.

The dust cloud along the horizon grew larger as the other vehicle rushed toward them.

Thirty seconds.

Adrenaline soared. He glanced at Bret. His skin was pale, but there was a resolute set to his jaw. They could do this. They had to do this.

Forty-five seconds.

He called back at Issa. "How much longer with the fuel?"

"Thirty...forty seconds."

Colton glanced back as the oncoming car came into view and felt his stomach knot. They didn't have thirty seconds.

"Water level's fine," Lexi said, slamming down the hood. "But I found something else. They strapped a cell phone to the inside of the engine."

"Why would they do that?" Bret asked, keeping his weapon steady on the oncoming car.

"They wanted to find you and knew you'd come back to the car," Colton said. "If they can trace the phone, they can trace us."

"They can do that?" Issa asked.

"They already did," Colton said. "They might be a band of opportunists, but they're also smart."

One minute. Colton kept his aim on the vehicle. They were running out of time.

A bullet pinged off the front bumper of their Jeep. Colton jumped back. There was no question any longer who had been following them.

"Everyone get back in the car," Colton shouted. "Issa? How much longer?"

"Almost done."

But there was no more time. He could see the passengers in the Land Rover. In another few seconds he'd be able to read the license plate.

Colton waited until the last second, when he knew he could make an accurate shot, and fired off a bullet, hitting the other vehicle's front tire.

The car spun out in a swirl of dust.

They'd just bought themselves some more time.

"Go...go...go..." Issa shouted at the two of them to get into the car as he tossed the now-empty jerry can into the back of the vehicle, then jumped into the driver's seat.

"Everyone okay?" Colton asked, as Issa started the engine, then slammed on the accelerator.

Bret and Lexi nodded. But while they all might be fine for now, this still wasn't over.

"Are they coming after us?" Issa asked, his gaze straight ahead.

"They're not moving," Colton said. "For now."

He pulled the battery out of the back of the phone Lexi had found and threw it out the window. "This is definitely how they found us."

Irritation burned through him. He was tired of the cat and mouse games. They needed to find a way to end this once and for all.

"They have to know we're headed for Morocco," Lexi said. "If they get that tire fixed they'll be after us again."

"Agreed," Issa said. "But I don't see any other options at this point. And there will be dozens of armed guards at the border. I can't see them trying anything there."

Colton wanted to agree, but these men were ruthless and didn't play by any rules. Plus they had no way to know whose pockets they had lined with bribes, or how far their influence reached. Issa believed they'd be safe crossing into Morocco, but what if he was wrong?

"What's this border like?" Lexi asked.

"It's typical for Africa. Passport checks, customs checks and vehicle searches," Issa said. "There will be armed patrol guards, along with a barrage of people bombarding you for money or trying to sell you something."

"But you still believe we'll be safe once we cross into Morocco?" she asked.

Issa hesitated a second too long, confirming his own uncertainty. "I believe so. But we've already discovered that these men have spread across the desert like a virus."

TWELVE

It felt as if they'd driven to the end of the earth. And they were still driving. Lexi glanced out the window of the 4x4 to where the terrain had changed little over the past couple hours. Mile after mile of sand dunes and desolate desert scenery surrounded them. The desert held its own kind of beauty that even she could appreciate. But after the last couple days trapped in its isolation, she was ready to leave.

Issa had told them that they were finally getting close to the border. Another fifteen, maybe twenty minutes, and they'd be there.

She glanced out the back window. There had been no signs of the car that had been following them, which brought a measure of relief, but she still wasn't convinced it was over. All she could do was pray that Colton's shot had damaged the other vehicle to the point where they hadn't been able to continue. But even if they weren't following them, there was still another huge hurdle to cross. Getting into Morocco.

"How long do you think the border crossing is going to take?" she asked, trying to settle her nerves.

"It's hard to predict," Issa said. "An hour...two...

maybe three. It depends on a number of factors. How many cars are already lined up, along with the mood of the border authorities."

"And the exact process?"

He'd gone over it briefly, but she needed to feel prepared. Or at least as prepared as she could.

"First we'll pass through the Mauritania side. Uniformed officers will ask to see your documentation. There are customs forms that have to be stamped, as well as the actual passports, and a fingerprint machine and photos for foreigners. Beyond that, there's a good chance they'll inspect our vehicle, and like with most border crossings, there will be plenty of determined people offering to help us in exchange for a fee."

"And me?" she asked. "What am I supposed to do? Simply walk across to the Moroccan side and hope they don't notice me?"

Issa glanced in the rearview mirror and caught her gaze. "That's always an option, but I think it's better if we tell them the truth up front. We can explain how you were the victim of a serious crime. You lost your passport, and are now headed to the American Embassy."

Lexi pressed her nails into the palms of her hands, still not convinced this plan was going to work. Not only did she need to make sure Mauritania allowed her to leave, she needed the Moroccan government to let her enter. Without any documents.

"And you think they'll believe me and just let me walk through without a passport?" she asked.

The last time she'd crossed one of the North African borders, she'd had to deal with two armed and hostile policemen, who'd pumped her with questions for the good part of an hour before finally letting her through. And that time, she'd had all her documents with her.

"There's no way to know, but I think Issa is right. I don't think we have a choice," Colton said. "Though I do have some cash in case we need to…persuade them."

Colton's words only stoked her fear. In case they needed to persuade them? Like if they threatened to arrest her for trying to cross illegally? Bribes were common, but technically illegal. What if they were able to pay off the authorities on one side but the armed guards on the other side couldn't be bought? Or Colton didn't have enough money to pay both groups?

"Once we get through the first border control and passport checks, we have to go through no-man's-land," Issa said, continuing his explanation.

"Isn't that where we are now?" she asked, with a chuckle.

"It might seem like it, but no-man's-land is a four-kilometer stretch of unclaimed desert between the two countries that is surrounded by land mines."

"Land mines?" Lexi glanced at Colton, unsure if she should laugh or cry. "This just keeps getting better and better. All I have to do is walk through the border without a passport while trying not to get blown up by a land mine, or get caught by Salif's men, who for all we know are still on our tail."

"The land mines exist all over the Sahara," Issa explained. "Many of the countries are too hostile toward each other to have their borders touch. So the no-man's-land is their solution. But there is no need to worry. As long as we stay on track, the road is easy to follow."

"And Salif's men…" she said. "Do you think they'll follow us across?"

"If Salif is smart, he'll realize it's time to give up." Colton said.

"Except the man's hardheaded," Issa said. "He might give up on the ransom attempt he organized himself, but Lexi's kidnapping is different. He was hired to find the money, and I have a feeling his reach might be farther than any of us realizes."

Lexi leaned her head back against the seat, closed her eyes and started praying. Letting her emotions swing out of control wasn't going to help anyone. She needed to draw from God's strength and focus on the fact that they were safe. That they'd managed to once again evade Salif's men. And while she might be a day or two later than she'd originally planned, she still might be able to make Micah's wedding.

She felt Colton's fingers wrap around her hand and opened her eyes.

"You okay?" he asked.

She looked at him, thankful once again for his presence and unwavering strength. If she had to deal with this on her own…

"For the most part. I just realized that my flight to Ireland was scheduled for today. My stepfather was going to get a hold of Micah and tell her what was going on, but when I spoke to him, I was supposed to be on my way out of here."

"We are on our way," he said.

"I know, but things have gotten a bit more…complicated." She bit back the tears. "I guess I'm not used to being kidnapped, chased and shot at."

She shook her head. Saying it out loud made it sound crazy. Like a lame line from some action movie script.

"You said Micah's fiancé's from Ireland?" he asked.

She nodded. "They're a very well-off family, and while I've only seen photos of the venue they chose, it's absolutely incredible. Three hundred acres of woods and lakes, along with a castle dating back to the thirteenth century. Talk about a fairy-tale wedding."

"We're going to get you there."

She shrugged her shoulders. "Somehow, dreaming of castles, rich food and a spa treatment seems completely frivolous right now. All I really want is a hot shower and some clean clothes."

"It's not frivolous—it's normal. Trust me, I have three sisters and each one of them spent what seemed like hundreds of hours planning their weddings. Of course none of them were married in a European castle, but I'm sure given the opportunity they would have jumped at it."

She smiled, but even his attempt to lighten the mood wasn't working. Not completely anyway. "I'm scared, Colton. I still don't know how this is going to end. If Salif's men show up behind us, or if they're waiting for us at the border…"

He squeezed her hand. "Isn't this how life always is? The unexpected hits us—job loss, sickness, financial issues—and we never know how it's going to end. Granted, this situation is way out of the ordinary, but in reality the only thing we ever know for certain is that God's still right here and none of what has happened over the last few days has surprised Him."

"I know." It was the one thing she'd continued to hang on to. Knowing that God was here even in the midst of tragedy, fear and pain. A passage from the Psalms played through her mind.

We will not be afraid, even if the earth is shaken and the mountains fall into the center of the sea...

"I've been impressed at how flexible you've been," Colton said, breaking into her thoughts. "I've seen how you're able to roll with the punches."

"It's not like I've had a choice." She laughed, wishing she didn't like him so much. But she did. His strength. His genuineness. His love for his family. His ability to make her smile even in the most difficult of situations.

The other thing that surprised her about the situation was that despite everything that had happened, she still had no regrets at coming here. She'd specifically sought out a place that would stretch her both physically and emotionally. In the end what she'd gained had far outweighed what she'd given. And even though it had been a long time since she'd felt that sense of *normal*—and she'd have preferred to skip these past few days—she'd still volunteer again in a heartbeat.

Maybe normal maybe comfortable—was overrated.

Colton studied Lexi's expression as they made their way to the border. He'd felt an attraction to her the first time they'd met in Timbuktu, but he'd never expected to have a chance to explore those feelings any further. In fact, he'd had no plans to fall for another woman. At least not for a long time. It was why he was here in Africa. To forget Maggie. Which was exactly what had happened. Maggie was—he could safely say—a thing of the past. But that didn't mean he was ready to jump into another relationship again. How was it then that he couldn't stop thinking about Lexi? Or that he wanted to figure out a way to get to know her better once this was all over? And yet that's exactly what he wanted.

"You mentioned that one of the reasons you came to Africa was to find closure from your mother's death?"

"I needed time and space to heal."

"Sounds like the two of you were close."

"Very. I miss her every day, but she's the one who taught me to always live life to the fullest and take chances. When she was diagnosed with cancer, she booked a month-long European cruise for her and my stepfather. She told me she wasn't done living and that there were still so many things she wanted to see and do." Lexi's gaze dropped, but there was a slight smile on her lips. "She rarely complained, always thought about others and never just talked about what she wanted to do one day. She did it. That's how I want to live."

"She'd be proud of what you're doing here."

"I hope so. And while I know it sounds horrible, I'm thankful she didn't have to go through all of this. Trent might have been her stepson, but she loved him like her own, and if she'd known what he was involved in, it would have broken her heart."

"We're almost there," Issa said, breaking into their conversation.

Colton looked outside as they passed a blue cargo container with Office of Tourism written on the side. He drew in a deep breath. He was determined to keep Lexi safe at any cost. They'd make it across the border, then head to the embassy on their way out of the country, where all of this would be behind them. He'd make sure she got to her friend's wedding, and then he'd find a way to see her again.

Or at least that's what he was going to keep praying would happen.

Issa pulled into a parking spot in front of a sand-colored building. There was a police car next to them. Colton looked behind them. There was no sign of the other vehicle that had followed them, which hopefully meant one less thing to worry about.

"We'll let you do all the talking, Issa," Colton said, as they exited the vehicle. "You up to this, Bret?"

He glanced at his brother-in-law who had been quiet for most of the trip. With a few good meals and some rest, he was going to be back to normal. He just needed to get Bret home. Needed to get all of them home.

"A few hours at the border in the sweltering sun?" Bret shot Colton a smile. "I've had worse days."

He couldn't help but smile back. They'd all had worse days recently. Which meant this was going to be a piece of cake. At least he hoped so.

An hour later, Colton decided that crossing into Morocco was going to be anything but simple. The sun pounded down on them relentlessly. He was worried about the constant jostling of people beside them begging for money or trying to sell cigarettes and cold drinks. He kept close to Lexi's side while Issa explained over and over to the authorities what had happened.

Maybe they should have tried to smuggle her across. Or maybe that would have made things worse. There was no way to know. She was strong, he knew that, but that didn't mean that the ongoing stress of the past few days wasn't affecting her. Because he knew it was getting to him.

He glanced behind them in the line. There was still no sign of Salif's men, but they were out there. Determined to get the two million dollars they'd lost as well as find Trent. And it wouldn't be hard to deduce where they were going. They needed to make it to the embassy and as far out of Salif's scope of influence as soon as possible.

But was Morocco going to be far enough?

He tried to dismiss the questions. All they needed to do right now was get into Morocco. From there on, they should be safe.

"They're taking too long," Lexi said, pacing beside him while Issa continued trying to convince the border officials to allow her to leave.

"They always take too long," he said. "It's part of the process."

"Maybe. And I know I shouldn't feel so much panic, but on the other hand I have been kidnapped—twice— over the past couple days, threatened and shot at…" She let out a huff of air. "I'm sorry."

"You have nothing to be sorry for." He reached into his pocket for some change, then haggled with a man for four Cokes. "Though this might help."

She took the drink, then shot him a smile, before taking a sip. "You're right. I don't think I realized how thirsty I was."

He handed one to Bret, then waited a couple minutes until Issa joined them to give him his drink.

"Anything?" Lexi asked.

"I'm trying to convince them to get someone from your government involved. The border patrol agent,

Nuru, told me to wait a few more minutes. There's actually a man here now who works for the American Embassy. Nuru's trying to track him down before he crosses into Morocco. If he's right—"

"They'll let me cross?" Lexi asked.

"That's what he implied."

For the first time all afternoon Colton saw hope in Lexi's eyes.

We just need a way across, God. And a way to put this nightmare behind us.

He stared past the line of cars toward the Moroccan border. A couple miles was all that stood between them and freedom. A couple miles and he could get Lexi through the disputed Western Sahara territory and on to Rabat, where she could catch a flight to Ireland and be done with this.

As Colton finished the last of his cold drink, a large African man wearing a dark gray uniform and accompanied by a second man approached them.

"I've been speaking with a colleague about your problem and might have found a solution," the man said, pushing his glasses up the bridge of his nose. "I would like to introduce you to Karim Fadel. He works for the American Embassy and has agreed to take you to the capital."

Issa quickly introduced Colton, Bret and Lexi to the two men.

"I'm returning from a business trip to Mauritania," Karim said with a thick English accent. "The Mauritanian official told of what you have been through. I'd be happy to help."

Colton hesitated briefly, before shaking the man's hand. It almost seemed too easy. Someone with the right credentials happened to be crossing at the same time they were and suddenly they are allowed to cross? He pushed back the thought and reached out and shook the man's hand. Why was he complaining? If it got the three of them across the border safely, that was all that mattered at the moment.

"Thank you. We appreciate your help tremendously," he said.

"It's the least I can do after what the three of you have experienced. The officials have told me they are going to allow you to leave Mauritania," Karim said, "And with my connections to the US Embassy, I don't expect any problems on the other side of the border once I explain the situation."

"Issa?" Colton said, before following the man to his car. "Are you coming with us?"

Issa's expression softened. "I'm sorry, but I won't be crossing into Morocco with you. I believe you are in good hands, and it will be better if I return home to my family."

"Are you sure?" Colton didn't like the idea of simply leaving Issa behind, but he wasn't sure there were any other options.

"What if they give you trouble back home?" Lexi added.

"I'll be okay," Issa assured them.

Colton prayed his friend was right as he gave him money for fuel and food for the return trip. "We owe you our lives, Issa."

"Then I will expect another visit to my home—from all three of you—though the next time I will expect to be under better circumstances."

Colton embraced the man. "Thank you, Issa. And please…be careful."

A minute later, the three of them were headed with Karim toward a silver Mercedes.

"I told you it was going to be okay," Colton said, nudging Lexi with his elbow.

"I guess I should listen to you more often."

"Yes, you should," he teased.

But despite his words, Colton still couldn't shake the sense of uneasiness. He looked back one more time as Issa slipped into his vehicle and drove away.

THIRTEEN

Forget the spa treatment Micah had promised her in Ireland. Standing in a bathroom, under a spray of hot water, in a traditional *riad* somewhere in the middle of a Moroccan neighborhood near the Atlantic Ocean, was the best shower Lexi could ever remember taking.

She finished washing her hair, thankful for their host's generosity in letting them stay the night. But as good as she felt physically, even the hot water couldn't wash away the fear still embedded in her pores.

A few minutes later, she was dressed in a simple tunic-styled dress Karim had found for her. She let the colorful fabric with its bright blues and oranges fall to the middle of her calves. It might not be something she'd typically wear, but it fit far better than the outfit Colton had found for her after the plane wreck. And carried fewer memories than the bloodstained pants she'd been wearing when the Malian army had shot the man standing next to her.

Would she ever forget everything that had happened to her?

Her hands shook as she picked up the glass of water she'd left on the counter. She might have lost her appetite, but she couldn't seem to get enough to drink. It was as if the heat of the Sahara had soaked up all the moisture in her body. She took a big gulp and moved to set it back down, but in the process the glass slipped from her shaky fingers and dropped onto the floor.

The cup shattered against the hard tile, echoing throughout the room like a gunshot. She was there again. Heart racing. Adrenaline flooding through her. Running for her life while the Malian government exchanged fire with her captors. Reliving the explosion of the surface-to-air missile that brought down the plane. Feeling the overwhelming panic as Salif's men shot at their vehicle in the desert.

She drew in a deep breath, pressed her back against the cool wall, then looked down at the floor. They could have killed her at any moment. One bullet could have snuffed out the life of anyone of them.

But this wasn't a bullet threatening to take her life. It was just a broken, replaceable glass. Not Salif's men or another car chasing after them across the desert.

She was safe. Far away from her captor and his men. Far away from the man who'd snatched her in hopes of finding her brother and in the process had changed forever how she looked at life.

Why, then, even though she was hundreds of miles from Salif, did she still not feel safe? She wasn't sure she ever would.

She glanced into the mirror, her heart still pounding. Another wave of fear swept through her, and she searched to find the source. She was alone for the first time since Colton had rescued her. But had the fear she felt really gotten that bad? So bad she couldn't even walk into a restroom by herself without panicking?

She studied her reflection. There were deep shadows beneath her eyes from the stress of the past few days. Her face seemed paler than normal. Her brain felt fuzzy to the point where she couldn't totally process everything that had happened. Maybe all of this was simply normal. Like a soldier coming back from war who'd seen things he'd only heard talked about.

But she was no soldier.

She pulled her wet hair into a high ponytail secured it with a band, then picked up the broken pieces of the glass off the floor before dumping them into a small metal trash can.

Colton had trained in the military and knew how to handle situations like this. She hadn't. She was trained to help people. To upgrade water systems so people could have clean water. Not to run for her life across the desert. And she had no idea how to deal with the aftermath of what had happened the past few days.

But maybe the truth was that the trauma was simply something she was going to have to live with. It was as if that part of her that had been violated, and taken against her will, had in turn managed to shatter the trust she'd always naturally felt toward others. Her mother had always called her a glass half-full kind of girl. She'd looked at the bright side of things—always expecting things to eventually turn out okay. Even after living in Mali these past few months and looking into the eyes of mothers desperate for their children's well-being, she'd still seen the hope for something better.

But during this experience—having to deal with the reality she'd almost died along with those around her—she'd lost a part of herself.

I don't know how to deal with how I feel, God. I have no idea how to go on from here.

No idea how to deal with the fear. The mistrust. The constant looking over her shoulder in terror that *they* were going to be there. She couldn't imagine feeling safe again, but she also didn't want to live in fear. She needed to get to Rabat, find her brother and seek closure. And then somehow she was going to have to figure out a way to put this behind her.

She hung up her towel on the rack behind the door, pushing to the back of her mind the continual flashbacks that refused to stop replaying. Trying to picture instead, those people who were thinking and praying for her right now. Her family. Micah. Colton...

Colton. He'd become her safety net. Her hero. And as crazy at it seemed, the thought of leaving Morocco without him terrified her. Almost as much as being alone. Not only had he been through most of what she'd experienced, but he'd managed to keep her safe each step of the way. And through the trauma, they'd bonded in a way she couldn't imagine possible. And now she couldn't envision saying goodbye.

But none of this—whatever *this* was—could last.

In the next day or two, they would go their separate ways. She was going to be on a plane to Ireland. She'd make it to Micah's wedding, and then on to see her family. He'd head to the East Coast. She'd eventually head to the West Coast.

And even she did decide to stay, chances were their paths wouldn't cross again for any significant period of time. Which was why there simply wasn't a place for him in her future. She knew that. But if that were true, then why did a part of her long for the chance to explore what she felt between them.

The muscles in her shoulders tensed. No. She might feel an unexpected connection to him. And even a need to be with him after everything that had happened. He'd become her security. But there could be no future for them. She'd learned her lesson with Evan. And she'd promised herself to never jump into another long-distance relationship. It simply didn't work.

Pushing aside her scattered thoughts for the moment, she stepped out into the hall and headed toward the roof, where Karim said they would be waiting for her with mint tea and cakes.

The outside of the house stood tall and had been made of a reddish stucco. Inside, there were bright colored tiles along the walls where most of the doors led to an interior courtyard. Any other time, she would have loved to explore the structure. But at the moment all she could think about was how vulnerable she felt. Every door had become a possible entrance for one of Salif's men. Every shadow a possible enemy.

She breached the stairs, then stopped at the top step. A dozen lanterns spread their yellow lights across the open-air rooftop revealing a cloth-covered rectangular table surrounded by wooden chairs and a number of couches adorned with colorful throw pillows. Bret sat at the table, looking relaxed as he drank a cup of tea next to a pile of small cakes. Colton stood with his back toward her, overlooking the view of the neighborhood and giving her a moment to compose herself. Because she didn't know how to ignore how she felt. Seeing him lessened the fear that continued to plague her. And caused her heart to race.

She greeted Bret, glad to see the color back in his cheeks, then walked over to where Colton stood along the edge of the terrace.

"Hey."

"Hey..." His smile broadened as he looked down at her. "How do you feel?"

"Better. I can't remember when a hot shower felt so good."

"I feel the same way."

Her heart skipped another beat as she looked up at him. There was no way to ignore the attraction she felt. The yellow light of the lanterns caught his clean shaven face and tall, muscular stature.

She felt herself relaxing, as if just being next to him could thwart anything evil that tried to come near her. Shifting her gaze, she looked out beyond the terrace dozens of windy roads lit up by streetlamps, while dogs barked and lively music played from someone's house.

"That's the Atlantic in the distance," Colton said, pointing into the darkness. "We're almost home."

Almost.

"It's a little different from the quiet of the desert," she said.

"Very."

"And Bret?" She breathed in the salty air from the sea mingling with the scent of roasting meat. "He's looking better, as well."

"He just told me he's feeling stronger. I think it's the fact that he'll be home soon."

She glanced up at Colton. His hair was still damp from the shower, and he'd changed into a pair of brown pants and a collared shirt. It was almost as if the last few days hadn't happened, and they were simply meeting for dinner at someone's home in the middle of Morocco.

"You look beautiful," he said, keeping his voice low enough that only she could hear him.

She felt a blush creep across her cheeks and wished he'd take back the compliment. He wasn't helping. She needed to put distance between them, not add to the unwanted feelings stirring within her.

"Our host has been generous," Lexi said, changing the subject. "Though I can't help but wish we'd been able to make it to the capital in one day."

"I know, but by tomorrow night we should be there."

"Did Karim mention trying to call our families again in the meantime?" she asked.

"I asked him just a few minutes ago when he was up here. He said the grid's still out."

Lexi swallowed her disappointment. She needed to call her stepfather and Micah and let them know where she was. To let them know she was okay and that this was finally over. "Seems strange that we were able to make a call in the middle of the Sahara and yet here in the city, the phones aren't working. How long does the system usually stay down?"

"Apparently not long. He said by morning everything should be back up again."

"I hope so." Lexi swallowed the frustration. But she could wait a few more hours. Because it wouldn't be long until they reached the capital and all of this was over.

Colton caught the hint of irritation in Lexi's voice. He couldn't blame her. He was just as anxious to get home. And at the least to make some phone calls and

let his family know he was okay. Becca needed to know
as well that this was finally over and she was safe to
go home.

But as thankful as he was that the last couple days
were over, there was one thing he wasn't looking forward to about going home. And that was the idea of
saying goodbye to Lexi. He studied her profile, wanting to know how she was really doing, but the lanterns
casting shadows across the rooftop terrace masked her
expression. But he didn't have to see her face clearly to
know she had to be dealing with a barrage of emotions.

Just like he was.

The imprint of shock never simply vanished just
because the situation was over. Even for someone like
himself who'd been trained to deal with trauma. Because no training completely prepared you for the consequences of war. For what happens on a subconscious
level when you pull the trigger on the enemy. Or for
how you would respond in a situation that left you feeling out of control and completely vulnerable. He had
his own memories of returning to the US after a call
of duty in the Middle East when he'd been treated for
symptoms of PTSD.

Lexi was going to experience a lot of the same signs
in the coming days and weeks and he felt this pull to
help her through it. Between being kidnapped and shot
at, she'd experienced as much as many of the soldiers
he knew. Living in a constant state of fear always left
a heavy mark psychologically. Which worried him.
He knew what trauma could do to a person. Knew
she needed to talk extensively to a counselor. But he'd
also seen her reach for that inner measure of strength

that was often hard to find. But she'd found it. She'd reacted amazingly well under the pressure she'd faced.

And she'd survived. They'd both survived. Making him want to extend their time together beyond Rabat. But instead, she was going to board a plane for Ireland, as he was boarding one for the US. Even if she returned to Mali to continue her work, the chance that they'd see each other again, or even every once in a while, was slim.

But was that even what he really wanted?

She brushed a loose strand of hair across her cheek as she stared out across the rambling neighborhood. Yes. Crazy as it seemed, that was exactly what he wanted. He felt as if he'd just scratched the surface of who she was and that in turn had left him wanting to dig deeper. She'd managed to stir something inside him that he'd tried to shut down since Maggie. Something he'd never expected to feel again. At least not anytime soon.

"Are you still planning to stop in Ireland on your way home?" he asked, breaking the temporary silence between them.

"I know my family is going to want to see me right away, but I can't imagine missing Micah's wedding. So yes. I'm hoping to take the earliest flight I can."

"I'm sure your family will understand. Just knowing you're safe is going to be enough for them until they see you."

"I hope so." She turned to him. This time he could see the worry marked across her forehead. "Can I ask you something?"

"Of course."

"Does the fear ever completely fade? Because while

my head tells me that we're going to be okay, my heart is still terrified. And even if it is all over, and I can really go home and live a normal life again, I don't think I'm every going to be able to look at the world again the way I used to."

He hesitated with his answer, knowing she didn't need him throwing some pat answer at her, by telling her that yes, everything was going to be fine.

"You're right," he said. "You'll never look at things exactly the same, but that's okay. And neither is there a *right* way to respond to a situation like this. There never is with things like fear and grief."

She ran her fingers across the fabric of her dress. "I knew life was going to be hard when I got here, and over the past few months I've seen things I couldn't even imagine seeing before. But this feeling of being violated. Of fearing that something else is going to happen. I don't know how to deal with the flashbacks and the panic. Or if they're ever going to go away."

Colton resisted the urge to pull her into his arms and hold her. Dealing with trauma was different for everyone. He'd watched soldiers lose everything after coming home, and others walk away without the experience seeming to affect them at all. But the reality was that no one who went through something like she had was going to walk away unscathed. Her entire sense of security had been shattered. Because this wasn't just an episode of some crime drama on TV. Her life had been threatened, her entire world upset, and those feelings weren't going to simply disappear overnight.

"What I do know is that you're going to need to make sure you take care of yourself and even more importantly give yourself time to heal. You're going to need the support of friends and family."

And he wanted to be part of that group that would be there for her.

I'm just not sure how to make this work, God.

"My stepfather's going to insist I see a counselor."

"That's not a bad idea."

"I know, but they're going to want to know details of what happened, and all I want to do is shove this entire situation behind me. Is it wrong to feel that way?"

"Like I said, there's no right or wrong about how you feel."

She looked up at him, and for a moment, he almost forgot Bret was sitting across the room. All he could see was the woman standing in front of him. And that he desperately wanted to kiss her.

"I'm sorry for the delay. I had some business."

Colton turned around, the sound of Karim's voice breaking into his thoughts. "My employer—and the owner of this house—would like to meet you," Karim continued. "He'll be up here in a minute. And in the meantime continue to make yourself at home."

"We appreciate everything you've done," Colton said, taking a step back from Lexi. "Though I thought you were employed by the US Embassy."

"I am. But only part-time as a consultant."

Another man stepped onto the terrace, wearing an expensive gray suit with a purple dress shirt.

"This is Adam Tazi," Karim said, making the introductions. "My employer and the owner of this home."

"I hope Karim has made you feel welcomed," Adam said.

"He has, thank you," Colton said. "The three of us are grateful for his help."

"Karim has kept me updated on your situation, and I understand you are all anxious to get to the capital." Adam stopped next to the table, picked up one of the small sweet cakes, then slowly popped it into his mouth. "Though there is one slight problem we need to deal with before we go."

Colton glanced at Lexi. "What kind of problem?"

"I understand that the three of you are acquainted with Salif."

"Salif... You know him?" Colton asked.

Adam smiled. "Quite well. In fact, I'm the one who hired him to kidnap your girlfriend here. Though the ransom demands for your brother-in-law were all his doing." He glanced at Bret. "I typically don't involve myself in things like that."

Colton heard Lexi's sharp intake of breath and took another step forward, trying to get his mind to wrap around what the man was saying. "Wait a minute. You're connected to Salif."

Adam frowned. "You can ask any of my friends, but I rarely joke. And never about something as serious as this."

Two more men carrying AK-47s stepped onto the roof and blocked the exit. Karim's friendly demeanor faded, as well, as he pulled out a 9mm handgun. Colton swallowed hard. How had he been so blind?

"I heard from Salif that the three of you have been quite innovative," Adam continued. "But please understand that things have changed. No one knows you're here. And no one is coming to your rescue."

"So your help at the border?" Lexi asked. "It was all a setup?"

Karim nodded. "It doesn't take much to bribe the officials. Sit down, both of you."

Colton hesitated, then grabbed Lexi's elbow and walked her to where Bret was waiting. They sat down on the cushioned bench, his mind already focused on finding an exit plan. But with three armed men plus Adam, the odds were once again against them at this point.

"Unfortunately for you, we're going to start again at the beginning." Adam stopped in front of Lexi and lifted up her chin with the butt of his gun. "Where is your brother?"

FOURTEEN

As Adam stared down at her, Lexi drew in a sharp breath, desperately wanting to wake up, once again, from the nightmare. The waves of panic were sucking her under. Adrenaline pulsed through her. Adam might not be Salif, but he'd already made it abundantly clear as far as she was concerned that he was far more dangerous.

"I asked you a question," Adam said. "Where is your brother?"

Her fingers gripped the edge of the bench beside him. "I told them earlier that I don't know where he is."

"That's too bad. Because if you want to live, then I will strongly suggest it's time for you—for all of you—to cooperate."

She glanced at Karim's weapon still pointed at them. How were they back where they'd started? And this time they'd walked right into the danger?

But regretting what they hadn't noticed wasn't going to change the situation. They needed a plan. A way to get out of this. Issa was hundreds of miles away, and they were still a day's drive from the embassy. They had no phone access. No GPS tracking device. Adam was right. No one knew where they were, nor did they have any way to communicate to let someone know they were in trouble. But that didn't mean she was ready to give up.

She looked briefly at Colton, knowing he'd do anything in his power to save her. But she couldn't simply rely on him. He and Bret were here because of her and what Trent had done. Which meant she had to help find a way out of this. And the only place she knew where to start was discovering what the man's next move was going to be.

"So this whole…kidnapping scenario," she began. "It's all about Trent and the money he embezzled?"

"You really are a smart girl."

She caught the sarcasm in his voice and wondered if she should shut up or continue to press for more information. Staying silent, though, wasn't going to give her the answers she wanted. "No one has told me exactly what Trent did."

Adam sat down across from them, his demeanor completely relaxed, as he grabbed another one of the tiny cakes off the platter. "These are delicious, aren't they? They make them fresh every day at a little bakery just down the road from us. Not quite as good as the Parisian bakeries, I suppose, or even the ones I've visited in New York. I discovered Italian doughnuts there."

Lexi frowned. It was as if they were sitting down for afternoon tea together. But she didn't miss what he was implying. He was telling her just how far his arm could reach.

"But I'm sorry. Where are my manners?" Adam said, brushing off his hands. "You were asking me about your brother. I'm surprised Salif didn't tell you."

"All he told me was that my brother had embezzled money from a business partner and that Salif had been hired to ensure he got it back."

"That business partner would be me." Any jollity in his voice had completely vanished. This was no game. "I'm assuming, then, as his sister, you know that Trent is a genius with numbers and computers. I was searching for someone I trusted who could set up a number of legally incorporated offshore corporations and then move my companies' profits around discreetly."

"You mean launder your profits?" Lexi asked.

Adam frowned at the comment, then apparently decided to ignore it. "What I didn't realize is that he's also a master manipulator. For the past couple of years, on top of moving my money to offshore accounts, he managed to create several bogus corporations through which he funneled funds—money stolen from my companies—into his own pocket."

"And the money he stole?" Lexi asked. "Where is it?"

"That is the million-dollar question, now, isn't it? I've got my best men on it and your brother didn't make it easy. He set up his personal accounts all over the world, too. Which is why I need him. He's the only one who can access them."

Assuming he still had the money.

A year ago he'd bought a new house in a pricey neighborhood north of LA. Six months ago it had been a new car. She'd never thought he was flashy with what he was earning, but he was spending. Now she knew how.

"I'm assuming that the phone lines aren't really down?" Colton asked.

"I couldn't exactly have you calling in the cavalry, now, could I?"

Lexi flicked a moth, attracted by the light above them, off her sleeve. "If that's true, then give me a phone, and I'll see what I can do to find him."

"I thought you didn't know where he was," Adam said.

"I don't. Not yet. But Salif never gave me the chance. If I can get some of his friends' numbers from my father, maybe I can track him down."

She glanced at Colton. She knew he was working to formulate an escape plan as they spoke, but if she could talk to her father and figure out a way to let him know where they were, there might be a way for the embassy to locate them and come up with a rescue plan.

"And then what?" Adam said. "You tip off the authorities as to where you are?"

"You're the one who needs to find my brother," she said. "If Trent hasn't responded to the video, he might this way."

"I don't know." Adam rested his hands against his thighs and leaned forward. "I'm beginning to believe the three of you are more trouble than you're worth. I'm half tempted to simply kill all of you and do this myself."

She felt a shiver race up her spine and knew she needed to choose her words carefully. "Except you can't do this yourself. You still need me."

Adam tossed a set of keys from his pocket at Karim. "Take them in the Jeep. And in the meantime, I'll give Trent forty-eight more hours to respond to the video."

"And after forty-eight hours?" Bret asked.

"You all will have proven to me that you have no value left."

* * *

Lexi felt the sharp jolt of the vehicle slam against her hip and winced at the pain.

Karim and his men weren't taking any chances this time. They'd secured their hands behind them and already she could feel the numbness in her thumbs spreading from the tight cord wrapped around her wrists.

She'd tried to pay close attention to where they were going, but keeping track of the turns had become impossible. And beyond the cracks of light coming from the edges of the blindfold they'd pulled tightly around her eyes, she couldn't see anything.

She felt the driver shift the vehicle into four-wheel drive and turn off the paved road onto a dirt one.

She also hadn't been unable to gauge how much time had passed. Which was disconcerting. She'd always a strong sense of time. Yet over the past few days, time had seemed to move in a completely different rhythm. And it was the same with details. Things she normally would have remembered, she suddenly couldn't.

Micah was a psychologist and had once spoken to her about the fallibility of witnesses' memories. Witnesses of the same crime often had a number of completely different testimonies with victims and bystanders remembering not only details that hadn't really occurred but also remembering things incorrectly. It was fascinating how human minds often filled in the gaps in what they remembered and interpreted due to fear, and the rush of adrenaline.

Lexi could relate. This situation had put her mind in a deep fog she didn't know how to escape.

She could feel the warmth of Colton's arm as he

bumped against her. Guilt mingled with fear. If it wasn't for her, Colton and his brother-in-law would be free. Bret would be back with his wife and son. Instead, their lives were again in danger.

"I'm sorry," she said, barely above a whisper.

"For what?" Colton asked."

"For all of this. This is my fault. The only reason we're here is because I didn't have my passport and we had to ask for help at the border. If we hadn't had to do that—"

"This isn't your fault, Lexi." He pressed his shoulder against her. "And you have nothing to feel guilty about."

She squeezed her eyes shut beneath the blindfold. She wanted to tell him he was wrong. That this was her fault, but there was nothing she could do anymore to try to fix things. Nothing she could do to make them all safe again.

The Jeep slowed down and came to a stop. The door next to her opened, and she could feel the butt of a gun press against her shoulder as she stepped out of the vehicle and into the darkness.

Colton opened his eyes and caught the yellow rays of light filtering through the one small window near the ceiling. Bret and Lexi were sleeping on thin mats beside him on the floor of the darkened room. He went to tug on the binding around his wrists, then remembered they'd taken them off when they'd left them here. There were no guards in the room, but that didn't mean there weren't any outside the thick wooden door in the far corner of the room. Apparently Adam was convinced there was no way to escape.

He was going to need to prove him wrong.

Colton got up off the mat, crossed the dusty cement floor, then pressed his hands against the door. It was solid and appeared to be bolted from the outside. Next, he moved around the inside perimeter of the room inch by inch. The walls appeared to be at least a foot thick, which meant while the construction seemed old, the structure was solid.

He stepped into the center of the room that held a few miscellaneous items like water jugs, a pile of discarded tires and a couple cardboard boxes, the room was empty. He looked at the window again, which seemed to be the only possible means of escape. It was too small for him, but if they could remove the bars, Lexi might be able to make it through. Shoving two of the tires next to the wall, he climbed up on the precarious ladder that made him just tall enough to look through the levers of semifrosted glass panes that were secured with rusty metal bars on the outside.

He shook his head and listened to the wind howling across the edges of the building, wondering what Adam was planning. Would he really kill them after the forty-eight hour deadline had passed? His gut told him yes.

"What can you see out there?"

Colton turned his head at the sound of Bret's voice. His brother-in-law was sitting up in the dim light, stretching his back.

"Looks like there's one other smaller building to the left, built into an embankment of sand. This one probably is, as well. Beyond that, it's just desert."

"So where do you think we are?"

Colton stepped down from his perch. "I've heard about deserted villages sprinkled across the desert.

There are supposed to be a vast expanse of secret trails and hiding places drug smugglers, human smugglers and other outlaws use to avoid being detected. This might be one of those places."

"It would make sense. Sounds as if we're definitely outside the city."

Colton nodded. "I agree, but we need to find a way out. We can't just sit here and wait the forty-eight hours."

"Do you have any idea what time it is?"

"The sun is sitting low above the horizon, so it must still be early." Colton glanced back at his brother-in-law. "Why don't you try and sleep some more?"

"I feel like all I've done the past few days is sleep. I want to do something to put a stop to this nightmare and get back with my family. We need to find a means of escape."

Colton nodded, but even if they did manage to get out of this building, chances were they were miles from help. He shifted his gaze to Lexi, who lay sleeping across the room. He knew she was exhausted. And knew the shock that was going to take hold when she woke up and realized that all of this hadn't just been a dream.

He watched her steady breathing. Her hair brushed against her face. She looked so peaceful and relaxed. All he wanted to do right now was to get her away from here. Not being able to do so made him feel helpless. But he was thankful that she was able to sleep. She needed to rest. There was no telling what was going to be ahead of them in the coming hours.

"You have feelings for her, don't you?" Bret said.

Colton's gaze shifted. He was too tired to deny how he felt. "It's that obvious?"

"Oh, yeah." Bret chuckled softly. "It's like watching a rerun of when Becca and I first met. I was completely smitten with her. I couldn't stop looking at her. I found every excuse in the book to talk with her and just be around her."

He wanted to deny the truth behind Bret's observation, but he knew he couldn't. "This isn't exactly the best scenario for getting to know someone, but Lexi... she's different."

"Different from Maggie?"

Colton sat down on the edge of the tires before answering. "I've tried not to compare them, but yes. She knew the risks coming here and yet she came anyway. Maggie would never move halfway around the world to help people she didn't know. I don't know how I missed just how different we really were."

Bret caught his gaze. "Why do I get the feeling there's a 'but' coming?"

"Because I can't forget Maggie. I keep thinking about how things ended between us. I don't want to go there again, and to be honest, how well do I really know Lexi?"

"You know she's beautiful, loyal, brave..."

"Is that enough?" Colton asked.

"It's enough for a start."

"Maybe. I just can't let it become a distraction. Not now. We need to find a way out of this, but how many times can we escape these people before our time runs out. I've checked this place over and it's locked up as tight as Fort Knox."

"And if we don't figure our way out of this?" Bret asked.

"Let's face it. They don't need us. Unless they decide to try for ransom money again, and we already know Becca can't come up with what they want."

No matter how he looked at things, it seemed like a no-win situation. And while he wasn't used to being a pessimist, he didn't know how to save them. Not this time.

"All I know is that when this is over, I think you need to pursue Lexi," Bret said. "Go out on a date like normal people do when they like each other, and then go from there. The two of you have a lot in common. A lot more than you and Maggie did anyway. All you just need is time to figure out how to make something work."

"Maybe."

"Because it's worth it, Colton. Finding the right person and falling in love." Bret clasped his hands in front of him. "I'm worried about Becca."

Colton turned away and studied a large crack in the wall that snaked across the bottom where the plaster had split. It was a subject he didn't want to talk about. He hadn't told Bret about the threats Becca and Noah had received. Or the fact that she'd gone into hiding, believing they were in danger. He hadn't wanted his brother-in-law to worry any more than he already was. Especially when there was nothing he could do.

"Colton…what is it?"

He debated for another few seconds what he should say, but trying to hide the truth at this point wasn't going to help. "I spoke to Becca back at Issa's place on his sat phone. You were pretty out of it that night with the pain from the scorpion bite, as well as from the medicine Sara gave you."

Bret leaned forward. "What did she say?"

"She got a phone call." He paused again, but there was no way of downplaying the significance of what she'd said. "They threatened to come after her and Noah—"

"Wait a minute." Bret stood up and began pacing in front of them. "Why didn't you tell me this before?"

"Because there was nothing we could do, and adding to your stress—"

"I deserved to know, Colton."

Colton glanced at Lexi, who stirred on her mat, unable to ignore the surge of guilt. Bret was right. He shouldn't have kept things from him.

"Please tell me there's no way they can reach Becca," Bret asked. "Is there?"

"I don't know for sure, but your kidnapping was Salif's idea. Not Adam's. And from what we know Salif's hold is just here in North Africa. And not even into Morocco. So he'd have to way of reaching Becca in the US."

Colton caught the anguish on Bret's face. He prayed he was right, but knew there was no way to be certain.

"If you're wrong, and Adam is involved in my kidnapping…" Bret shook his head, looking unconvinced. "He owns an international business whose reach definitely stretches to the US."

"All Adam wants is the money Lexi's brother stole," Colton said, trying to convince himself that Becca was safe as much as Bret.

"If that were true, then why am I still here? Why

are you still here? They can't use us as leverage when it comes to Trent."

"I can't answer any of that."

Bret combed his fingers through his thinning hair. "So you have no idea where she is or how to get a hold of her?"

Colton caught the panic in Bret's voice. "She's smart, Bret. She gave me the number of a burn phone where she can be contacted. I've got it scribbled on a piece of paper in my pocket."

"So she's gone off the grid." He let out a huff of pent-up air.

"No credit cards. No cell phone tracking. She's also been in contact with the agent from the FBI who's been handling your case from the beginning."

"So that means she's safe."

Colton nodded. Even if it meant their own lives were disposable.

Lexi stirred again, then sat up. He turned and read the confusion on her face as she looked around the room.

"Lexi...you're okay." He knelt down next to her. "We're all okay."

For now.

"I remember the guns, the ride in the vehicle..." She rubbed the back of her neck. "Where are the men who brought us here?"

"We don't know. They locked the door and left."

"And they haven't come back?"

"No."

She looked up at him. "I'm so sorry."

"For what?"

This..." She waved her hand. "This is all my fault.

All my brother's fault. And now the two of you are involved. You should be home with your wife right now, Bret."

"Forget it," Bret said. "I've tried the whole guilt thing with Colton. It doesn't work on him. And besides that, he's got this thing for rescuing damsels in distress."

Lexi looked up at him. "Okay, then how do we get out of this mess? I don't think Trent's going to come forward. He's probably taken the money he stole and is already living it up in some nonextradition country."

If she was right, he didn't like where that left them. They had no way of escape and no leverage. Or maybe Adam was going to go ahead with a ransom demand as plan B. What did he have to lose? Three foreigners. Two who held American passports. Maybe he thought they were a guarantee that he'd get at least a big chunk of his investment back.

Colton frowned. That had to be his plan. Because if not, he and Bret would already be dead. But either way, they needed to find a way out of this place before their captures returned and decided their fate for them.

FIFTEEN

Despite Bret's reassurance that she wasn't at fault, Lexi didn't know how to shake the guilt. But she also knew that homing in on that guilt wasn't going to help either. What was done was done, and while she couldn't change the past, Trent's actions, or even Adam Tazi's actions, she could help come up with a plan that would get them out of here. Frustration was fueling her anger, and she already knew she was going to need every ounce of courage she could muster.

Because she wanted to be more than just a damsel in distress. Though there was something terribly romantic about the days of chivalry, maidens and knights in shining armor coming to the rescue. If she was going to survive this, she couldn't imagine anyone she'd rather have at her side than Colton. And it was more than just the way he made her heart stir and her longing for the possibility of something more with him. She'd also come to trust him completely. His instincts were spot-on and his resourcefulness had saved her life more than once.

She stared at a dark spot on the floor where something had stained the cement. Even he couldn't completely erase her fear. But none of that changed the reality of what they were facing. For now, she just needed to focus on getting out of here. Nothing more.

"So what do we do?" she asked finally.

"The room's solid and built for the heat, which is why the walls are at least a foot thick," Colton said. "The two weakest points are obviously the door and the window, but even they come with their own challenges. The door is solid, but with some work it might be possible to take off the hinges. As for the window, the bars are old and rusty, which means we might be able to break them off."

Lexi frowned. Even with the room's weaknesses, it seemed that Adam had found the perfect place to keep them out of the way."

"So assuming we get out, then what?" she asked.

"We're far enough outside the city that all I could see from the window was desert."

Which meant they could be anywhere. She was certain they'd driven on the unpaved road for at least forty-five minutes, possibly an hour. They could easily be fifty or sixty miles from the outskirts of the city.

"I say we worry about what to do when the time comes that we get out," Bret said. "But I also think we need to stay ready for when they do show up. Because that's something that will definitely happen."

"Agreed." Colton stood as if he were preparing for a battle. "They'll be armed, but if we could take them off guard, we might be able to secure the advantage we need to subdue them."

"And get one or more of us shot." Lexi's frown deepened. She agreed that they should stay proactive, but that didn't make her feel any more comfortable with the idea of trying to take down armed captors. What were the odds of all three of them walking out alive?

What were the odds of all three of them walking out alive if they did nothing?

The thought sent a chill down her spine. Even if Trent did show up, Adam had no motivation for keeping any of them alive. They were now witnesses. They'd been to his home and seen his face. They knew too much for him to let them simply walk away.

"Lexi?"

She nodded at Colton. "I know you're both right. I've just never been in a situation where I had to fight for my life."

"I'll start working on the door hinges," Bret said. "Why don't the two of you try to break those bars off the window?"

She moved beside Colton next to the pile of tires under the window. "What do you need me to do?"

"We're going to have to come up with a sturdier ladder," he said.

"There's a couple boards in the back corner that might help stabilize it."

They spent the next few minutes in silence, working together to ensure their access to the window wasn't going to come crashing down on them. Once the makeshift ladder was finished, she volunteered to stand next to it to guarantee it didn't shift while Colton climbed on top of the pile to further examine the rusty bars.

"It's funny how all the things I used to think were so important suddenly don't seem to matter quite as much as they used to." She leaned slightly against the tires, watching for any movement as Colton balanced above her, and needing to verbalize some of what she was feeling. "Even some of the things I was looking forward to...somehow they seem so insignificant."

"Like your trip to Ireland?"

"Yeah." She couldn't help but wonder what Micah was doing right now. With only a few days left till the wedding, she knew there would be a flurry of activity. Which was why she had planned to arrive a few days early. Not only to see some of the sights of a country she'd always wanted to visit, but to help Micah with some of the last-minute details they'd discussed over the past few weeks.

"Will you hand me one of those pieces of card-board?" Colton interrupted her thoughts, bringing her back to her present situation—to a place somewhere in the Sahara. "I need to pull out these glass panes, hopefully without breaking them, in order to get to the bars."

He carefully pulled out the first pane, then set it onto the cardboard piece she was holding. "I don't think any of what is going on now should diminish what you were looking forward to. It simply puts things in a different perspective for the time being."

"It's hard to believe she's getting married in a castle in Ireland." Lexi let out a low laugh. "Can't really think of a place any more different than this."

"Where did they meet?" Colton asked, handing her the last pane.

"At a conference back in the States. It was pretty much love at first sight. At least for Micah. They got engaged right before I came to Africa. She's spent the past few months sending me everything from ideas to bridesmaid dresses to the font on the place cards."

It was going to be Micah's fairy-tale wedding.

"I'm still counting on getting out of here so we can get you there on time," Colton said.

She looked up at Colton and caught his gaze, wishing he was right. But at the moment, Ireland and Micah's fairy-tale wedding seemed a million miles away.

"What about the bars?" Bret said, walking across the room to where they were working.

"I've just got the glass off. Looks like there are a couple weak points, though without the proper tools this isn't going to easy."

"I found a long nail in the corner I've been using to try and loosen the hinges, but yeah, neither project is going to be easy."

Lexi heard the roar of a vehicle outside. Her fingers gripped the edges of the cardboard holding the glass.

Colton jumped down from the top of the tires. "So much for our forty-eight hours to prepare."

Any plan they'd had to escape vanished. She could hear the car doors slam shut, then a lock being turned. The door Bret had been working on opened.

Someone shouted for them not to move. A second later, she felt her eyes burn as the room filled with smoke. As the haze cleared, she saw two African men rush into the room, but it was the third man that caught her attention.

Lexi felt the blood drain from her face as the glass panels she'd been holding crashed to the floor. "Trent?"

Colton's eyes burned as he covered his mouth and nose with the palm of his hand. The room was full with a thick smoke, and he'd heard at least one shot. Using grenades or flash bangs were a common practice for the military in an ambush situation. It allowed them to return fire on the enemy while staying concealed so they could execute offensive maneuvers.

His mind raced through their limited options. Because while he and Bret both had military experience, in this scenario they were at a severe disadvantage. Not only did they not have the element of surprise, from what he could see through the smoke they were up against three men, and at least one was armed.

And there was an unexpected variable he wasn't sure how to calculate into the scenario.

Lexi had called out to Trent.

His jaw clenched, knowing he couldn't think about that right now. Now that the door was open, this was their chance to get out. He needed to level the playing field, and the only way to do that was for them to quickly change positions and attempt to regain the element of surprise.

Unless she'd already moved, Lexi was now behind him and to his left. Bret had been near the door to his right. He shifted left where he could see the subtle outline of one of the men. Even taking down one would be a start at tipping the odds in their favor. He needed to not only disarm the man, but disable him, as well. At least the smoke put both sides at a disadvantage.

Colton heard a shuffle to his right, then Bret cried out. But Colton couldn't give his position away by calling out to his brother-in-law to see if he was okay. The smoke began to clear just enough for him to see a man coming at him with a small handgun. His choices in defense had to be adjusted when there were weapons involved. Disarming him could prove to be too risky, but at this point, his options were few. He reacted immediately, shoving the man's hand away from below in order to deflect his aim. Half a second later, Colton pushed back his arm to ensure his attacker was unable to use his weapon. Wincing in pain, the man dropped the gun onto the ground. Colton aimed for the windpipe, then used the momentum of his own body to drop the man onto the ground.

In a matter of seconds, the exchange was over. His attacker stared up at Colton from the cement floor.

Colton looked around. The air in the room was finally beginning to clear. He saw that Bret had managed to take down one of the intruders, as well.

"Are you okay?" he asked, ignoring the assailant for the moment.

"I'm fine. But where's the third man?"

Colton tried not to panic. "Where's Lexi?"

"Lexi!" He shouted out her name, but there was no answer.

Another wave of panic seeped through him. Besides the four of them, the room was empty. Had this been the plan all along? A distraction to ensure they got her?

Colton turned back to the guy he'd just taken out. He picked up the man's gun and aimed it at his heart. Blood ran from the assailant's nose and down his face from where Colton had hit him.

"Where did he take her?"

"I don't know. Her leaving wasn't part of the plan."

"Then what was your plan?"

The man's jaw jutted out in defiance, his lips pressed tightly together as he turned his head.

Colton pressed his boot against the man's shoulder as added encouragement.

He winced in pain. "Okay... We were supposed to let him see that his sister was alive, then he was going to give us the account numbers for the money he'd stolen. The smoke was to ensure we weren't ambushed when we entered the room."

"Looks like your plan didn't work," Colton said, but he wasn't sure what had actually transpired. Had Trent grabbed his sister in all the commotion? "What were you supposed to do with us when this was over?"

"Kill you."

Colton felt his gut tense. So there had never been any intentions of any of them walking out of here alive.

"Colton Landry?"

Six heavily armed men wearing fatigues rushed through the door and into the lingering smoke. Colton shifted his weapons and aimed it at the lead intruder's heart.

"Stop right there—"

"Slow down." One of the men held up his hand. "We're on your side."

Colton noted the USA patch on his uniform, but even with the familiar insignia, he wasn't ready to blindly trust anyone again. "Who are you?"

"Lieutenant Samuel E. Stevens. US Army. We were sent here to take you back to the capital." The man's gaze shifted to the floor. "Though it doesn't look like you need us now."

"There was a third man, who escaped," Colton said. "And he took Lexi Shannon, the woman who was with us. We believe the man was her brother. She never would have left on her own."

"Trent Hudson," the lieutenant said.

Colton nodded. "Lexi's stepbrother."

The lieutenant signaled to two of the soldiers to handcuff the men on the ground.

Colton stepped up to the lieutenant. "Tell me what's going on."

"We arrested Mr. Hudson in a hotel room in the capital, and after some persuasion he eventually agreed to help us find you. He was fitted with a tracking device so we could keep tabs on him at all times," the lieutenant said. "That's how we found you."

"And the Moroccan government," Bret asked. "What are they doing here?"

"This ended up being a joint operation between their government and ours. We wanted our hands on Adam Tazi, who's on the FBI's most-wanted list for dealing weapons and a long line of other felonies. The Moroccan government wanted him caught for crimes in this country. Trent made a deal with the FBI. A lower sentence for his involvement with Adam Tazi's enterprises if he helped us capture the man and help us to find you."

"And did you find Tazi?" Colton asked.

"We arrested him on our way here."

"Well, apparently Trent backed out on your deal, because he's gone and so is his sister." Colton frowned. His least concern at the moment was Trent. They needed to find Lexi. "What about the tracking device he was wearing? We need to find them."

As he stepped out of the room and into the blistering sunlight behind the lieutenant, one of the soldiers walked toward them and announced that Trent had dumped the tracking device.

Colton tried to control the alarm he felt. The rotors of a helicopter pulsed in the distance. But there was no sign of Lexi or her brother.

"We can still find him." The lieutenant spouted off

a string of instructions into his radio. "There's only one main road out of here back to the city. We've got a local ground team right behind us. The only reason we didn't wait to go in is because we realized you were under attack. But my men will find them."

"And in the meantime?" Bret asked.

"We're going to get you out of here." He called out orders to one of his men. "The helicopter will take you to Rabat."

Colton hesitated at the offer. There was no way he was going anywhere without Lexi. Trent might be her family, but Colton was certain that her safety wasn't one of his priorities. He'd already double-crossed the government despite whatever deal they'd made, not to mention the money he'd embezzled from his boss. Trent Hudson wasn't a man to be trusted.

"Let my brother-in-law go with the helicopter. He's going to need a thorough medical exam once he gets to the capital, but I'm coming with you."

"My orders were to get both of you back to Rabat," the lieutenant said above the roar of the helicopter rotors.

Colton bit back a sharp response. He understood the lieutenant's position, but as far as he was concerned, this wasn't a negotiation. He was staying, with or without the soldier's permission. "After two tours of duty in Afghanistan, I know how to handle myself."

"You did bring down Adam's men with no firepower. That's enough to impress any of us."

"I'll see you in Rabat, then." Colton grabbed his brother-in-law into a tight bear hug and said goodbye before heading back with the lieutenant for the three

Land Rovers that had just arrived. "You know Trent was never planning to come back with you."

"What do you think he's doing, then?"

"I think he took Lexi as leverage. A guarantee that he could escape across the border into Spain and disappear without getting shot."

"He'll never make it."

"You can't be sure of that. He's got Lexi, the funds and the motivation with nothing to lose at this point."

The lieutenant pulled open the driver's door to the Land Rover. "Then let's make sure he doesn't make it."

SIXTEEN

Lexi bit the edge of her lip as Trent sped across the sand in the stolen Land Rover. She'd expected Adam's men to return, but she'd never expected this. Her lungs still burned from breathing in the fumes from the smoke bomb, but her heart hurt more. She never imagined her own brother would stoop to kidnapping her.

"I'm sorry, Lexi." Trent finally broke the silence between them.

Sorry? He had no idea what his actions had put her through the past few days. Sorry couldn't begin to make up for what he'd done.

"If you're sorry, then tell me what's going on." She glanced at him, but he kept his eyes on the road straight ahead of them. "Tell me what you're doing here, why you took me and why we left Colton and Bret back there."

His fingers tightened against the steering wheel. "You'd been taken hostage. I'm your brother. What did you expect me to do? They would have killed you."

"Don't even start to play games with me, Trent."

"Their orders were to kill you."

She didn't believe him. Because it was just another

lie. She knew him well enough to be certain he hadn't come all this way just to rescue her. With him there was always a hidden agenda. Whatever his motivation was, she knew it was a selfish one.

"I know about the embezzlement and the lengths Adam is willing to take to recover his money." Lexi leaned back against the headrest. She was tired and achy and wanted to go home, but first she needed to convince him to stop whatever he was trying to do. "I want to know what your plan is now. You do have one, don't you?"

"Those men back there…they're involved in a lot of highly illegal things."

"And from what I understand, so are you. Why did you really come with them, and where are we going now?"

"It was my only way out, selling out both sides. And I needed some kind of guarantee that I could leave the country and get into Europe without getting shot on sight."

"So you took me."

"I'm sorry to have to involved you—"

"No, you're not." She reached up to scratch her arm, then drew in a sharp breath, temporarily shoving Trent's betrayal aside. Blood had seeped through the sleeve of her dress and was running down her arm. "Trent…"

"What's wrong?"

"I don't know." She pulled her hand away. It was covered with blood. "I don't remember getting hurt."

Neither had she felt any pain. Maybe it was because of the adrenaline, but now that she saw the trail of blood dripping down her arm, she could feel the intense sting of the wound slicing through her like a hot knife.

"You must have been shot," Trent said.

"Shot?" She shook her head. "That's not possible." Or was it? She'd heard at least one gunshot.

"There's probably a first aid kit in here somewhere," Trent said. "Look in the glove compartment and under the seat. If nothing else, you need to stop the bleeding."

She started looking, but that wasn't all she needed.

"We need to go back, Trent." She felt under the seat with her fingers, then pulled out a small first aid kit. "We have to get help. And I need to make sure Colton and Bret are okay."

Trent pressed his foot against the brake, stopping the vehicle, then grabbed the kit from her. "Forget it. We're not turning back. But let me at least try to wrap your arm up."

She felt the muscles in her back and shoulders tense as he opened up the box and pulled out a compress dressing and a small roll of tape. Her heart was racing. Since when was she afraid of her own brother? Saying nothing, she felt the burn of the injury as he pulled up her sleeve, then pressed the dressing against her arm.

"It's just a surface wound. You'll be fine."

Except she wasn't fine.

"Tell me why you're here. Why we're here," she said.

"Long story short, I struck a deal with the FBI. But it didn't take me long to realize that while I don't want to face the retribution from Adam and his men, I also don't want to be stuck in prison for the next decade." Trent ripped off the tape and made sure the makeshift bandage was secure. "So I took the third door, which will hopefully land me on some tropical island some-where completely off the grid."

"And in the meantime, you don't care who gets hurt?"

Trent finished bandaging her up, then dumped the first aid kit on the floorboard in front of her and started driving again. "If you're talking about your friends back at the compound, then you'll be happy to know that the US military were right behind me. If all went according to plan, which I'm sure it did, they arrested Adam and his men."

"How did they know how to find us?"

"They fitted me with a tracking device so they could follow me."

"And I'm guessing you ditched the device?"

"You bet I did."

Lexi worked to put the pieces of the puzzle together. At least there was a chance that Colton and Bret were okay. "So why is our military showing up now?"

"Adam Tazi's on the FBI's Most Wanted list. That's pretty good motivation. Made striking a deal with them easy."

"And you?" she asked. "What do they want with you?"

"Somehow my name got connected with Tazi and my passport was flagged." Trent fought to stay in the ruts of a stretch of soft sand. "I never meant to hurt you, Lexi. You have to believe that. I honestly never thought Adam would involve you in this."

"So you didn't think there would be consequences to stealing money from a man wanted by the FBI?"

"It wasn't supposed to end this way. I was going to disappear. Start over somewhere on the other side of the world and no one would get hurt. It's not like Adam doesn't have millions coming in far and beyond what I took."

"But people did get hurt, and I got caught in the cross fire." Literally. "I don't understand how you thought you could simply disappear?"

"That was—and still is—my plan. When I came to see you, I didn't think he'd connect us. I never talked about you, and we have different last names. I needed a place where I'd be safe until I could finish clearing the money and work out the details to disappear."

"What about your father? What's he going to think when you end up in prison?"

"Like I said. I have no intention of going to prison. Not even at a reduced sentence. That's why I have you. All I need is a second chance to start over and put all of this behind me."

Lexi shook her head. Her arm was beginning to throb along with her head. She reached for the first aid kit, needing something for the pain, but even more, needed a way to get through to her brother.

Didn't he understand that there was no way he was going to be able to simply walk into Spain with a marked passport? And if—when—the FBI took him back into custody, any deal he'd made with them was already off the table.

She found an individual package of Tylenol and managed to swallow them without water. "You'll never make it."

"What do you mean?"

"You'll never make it across the border. And even before that, you'll have to deal with the frequent police checks on the main road. They'll demand passports.

Yours is marked and I don't have one. And then what? But if you turn yourself in now—"

"Forget it, Lexi. Because I have connections. There are people who you can pay to smuggle you across the border. It's the connection I was working on before all of this went down. I'll get a new identity and disappear, and you won't have to put up with my indiscretions anymore."

She glanced over and caught the determined set of his jaw. "What happened, Trent?"

"What do you mean? How did I go from being the black sheep of the family to a wanted criminal?" He shook his head. "It's easier than you think. You see an opportunity—right or wrong—and you decide to take it. Eventually you end up where I am."

"There's always a way out—"

"Don't start preaching at me. My dad did enough of that over the years."

"Maybe, but there are always choices."

He'd never been one to listen to anyone else. He'd always preferred to learn the hard way. But this time his decisions might very well have cost him everything.

Five minutes later, he pulled onto the main road and headed north. She knew they were five, maybe six hours from the border of Morocco and Spain. What she didn't know was where Colton and Bret were. Because despite Trent's assurances, she didn't even know if they were alive. The men who'd set off the smoke bomb had been armed. And even with Colton's military experience, the odds against them had been high.

"So what happens now?" she asked, breaking the silence.

"You come with me to the border as my insurance

policy until I can disappear into Europe where I've got someone waiting to pick me up. It will be a lot easier for me to hide there than it is here."

"What about me?"

"Assuming everything goes as planned, and no one tries to stop me, you can head back to Morocco. There are always foreigners driving down who can give you a lift."

So this was how it was going to end? With him dumping her off at the border of some third-world country while he disappeared? At least it would be over. Though that hung on a very big *if* they even made it there.

Lexi studied the road ahead of them, then looked at Trent. Just as she'd said, there was a blockade with uniformed police.

"Trent…"

"It's not a big deal. Most of the time they just wave people on."

He might sound in control, but she didn't miss the edge in his voice.

"And if they don't?" she asked. "If they stop you and ask for my passport?"

"I don't want to hurt you, Lexi." He pressed his lips together, then lowered his voice when he spoke again. "I'm sorry. But please. Don't test my patience. Because I'm going to get out of this country one way or another, and I'm not afraid to do whatever it takes to make that happen."

She felt her mouth go dry, unable to speculate if he would actually follow through with his threat as one of the uniformed police officers holding an AK-47 stepped out into the road and signaled for them to stop.

* * *

Colton caught himself tapping his fingers against his leg in the front seat of the Land Rover. He flattened out his hand. He needed an outlet for his nervous energy. No matter what had happened back there, he felt responsible. Lexi had counted on his protection and yet he'd been unable to stop her from vanishing.

"How long till we get to the main road?" he asked the lieutenant, who had taken the wheel and was driving as fast as he could across the sand back toward the coast.

"A couple miles at the most."

He started tapping again. The problem was that once they got to the main road there was no way to say for certain if Trent had headed north or south. Or if he'd decided to hunker down in the city until things quieted down.

He dismissed the last idea immediately. Trent was smart he would want to get as far away from the authorities as possible. Which left the other two options. But even then, only one was truly viable. Heading south would take him down into the Western Sahara and Mauritania. If he were Trent, Colton would head north then take a ferry out of Tangier, a Moroccan port city on the Strait of Gibraltar, or for the right price, he could even pay someone to smuggle him across the eight mile stretch of shipping lanes into Spain.

"Which way are you planning on heading once we get to the main road?"

"Without the tracking device it's going to be impossible to know for sure, but the logical choice is to go north."

"Agreed," Colton said, glad they were thinking the same thing. "But if Trent doesn't go in that direction?"

"We'll still find him. The man's got nowhere to run. And on top of that we're working closely with the Moroccan authorities, who want to find Adam Tazi's entire network just as much as we do."

A minute later, they turned onto the dusty main road. Stones bounced under the wheels as the lieutenant maneuvered his way through the edges of town, past camels, donkeys and herds of goats. Trucks crawled north with oversize loads next to long lines of schoolchildren walking along the road on their way home. Soon the business of the city gave way to stretches of rust-colored earth with clumps of grass and plants in the distance, along with lone, stone houses, earthen mosques, olive groves and copper mines.

But the details of the surrounding scene blurred together as Colton focused on only one thing. They had to find Lexi.

"What's your connection with Lexi Shannon?" The lieutenant's question broke into Colton's thoughts. "I've only heard parts of your story, including your brother-in-law's kidnapping. But even from the little I do know, it's obvious the three of you have had a rough few days."

"That's an understatement." Colton let out a low laugh, but the worry gnawing at him over Lexi's disappearance only grew. He had no idea how Trent was going to react in a situation like this, but the man had chosen to walk away from a deal the FBI had offered him that would have lessened his time in prison. If he got caught at this point, Colton assumed that the FBI wouldn't uphold whatever agreement had been made

between them. Which meant Trent was desperate not
to get caught.

"Bret was kidnapped two months ago and his kidnappers demanded two million dollars," Colton began.
"Knowing there was no way we could come up with
the money, I ended up making a deal with the Malian
government. And our plan worked. Sort of. At least
until my plane got shot down as we were leaving."

"Wow... You took quite a risk."

"I didn't exactly have a lot of options. As for Lexi,
she'd been abducted the day before and was being held
at the same place as my brother-in-law."

"These kidnappings for ransom are a no-win situation," the lieutenant said, passing a large truck filled
with propane tanks. "When the ransoms are paid they
become a huge source of funding for terrorist groups,
which governments can't encourage, and yet when people's lives are at stake it suddenly becomes a complex
and serious matter that just can't be ignored."

He was right. There was no easy resolution.

The lieutenant glanced at him. "We'll find her. I
promise. There's no way they'll get far. The police have
their descriptions and this country's full of speed traps
and checkpoints."

Colton nodded, but the man's assurances didn't
erase his anxiety, or his urgency to find Lexi. He didn't
know Trent beyond what Lexi had told him, but if he
was desperate enough to escape both Adam Tazi and
the FBI, how far was he willing to go to secure his
freedom?

SEVENTEEN

Colton's heart beat faster as he listened to the lieutenant's side of a phone conversation thirty minutes later. He wasn't able to decipher what was going on but he hoped it was good news. Communications, even on a government level, were never swift on this continent, but in this situation the Moroccan government had as much on the line as the US government. All he could do now was pray it was going to be enough.

"They found them," the lieutenant said, hanging up the phone and dropping it into his lap. "I knew there was no way they could go far."

"Where?"

"At a checkpoint just ahead of us."

Two minutes later, he could see a couple of vehicles pulled over along the side of the road and several uniformed officers. But no sign of Trent or Lexi.

"Where are they?" Colton asked.

He studied the scene, looking for Lexi. His question was answered seconds later. Trent stepped out of one of the vehicles, dragging Lexi with him from behind. And he had a weapon pointed against her head.

A sick feeling sliced through Colton. He grabbed the

door handle and jumped out as soon as the lieutenant brought their vehicle to a stop. Because Trent had just answered another one of Colton's question. Clearly the man was willing to do anything, even use his sister as a hostage, in his search for a way out.

How has it come to this, God? He's her brother.

While the lieutenant quickly conferred with the Moroccan police, Colton searched Lexi's face and found a mixture of fear and shock. She'd known Trent was desperate, but this—he knew she'd never expected this.

Beside him, the lieutenant and his men had their weapons trained on Trent. If Lexi's brother didn't stand down, there was no way this was going to end well.

"What's going on, Trent?" The lieutenant took a step forward, turning his full attention on her stepbrother. "I was told you made a deal with the FBI. Your testimony for a lesser sentence. It was a very good deal, but now…now you're about to blow everything. What do you think the FBI is going to say when they find out you're holding your own sister hostage? I can promise you the deal's going to be off."

"Forget all of that. I'll still end up in prison," Trent said. "Which is why this time you're going to play by my rules. I'm going to need the keys to one of your vehicles. The two of us will drive away from here without being followed. And as long as no one tries to stop me, I'll leave Lexi—safe—at the border."

"Sorry, but that's not going to happen. I have orders to ensure this ends here, right now, without anyone getting hurt."

"Well then, I guess I'm going to have to disappoint you, because I have no intention of coming with you."

"And you think you'll be able to make it all the way to the border with a hostage?" the lieutenant asked.

"I have resources at my disposal." Trent moved Lexi in front of him and shook his head. "Call your boss. Tell him I need my demands met, or I will shoot her."

"She's your sister."

"My life is on the line as much as hers. And we all know that there are times when sacrifices have to be made."

Sacrifices? Colton stepped up next to the lieutenant. This was no sacrifice. These were the words of a man who'd lost touch with reality.

Colton turned to the lieutenant. "Let me talk to him."

The other man frowned. "You have experience in hostage negotiation?"

"In Afghanistan." He didn't need to know that it had only been one time. That didn't matter right now. He knew more about Lexi and Trent than the lieutenant. "Please. Just let me try."

"You're too close to the situation." Colton was about to argue when the lieutenant nodded. "But go ahead."

Colton stepped forward. "My name's Colton Landry. I don't work for the government, which means I can't make a deal with you, but I might be able to help."

"I doubt it, but my sister has told me about you. The military hero who saved her life. Sorry you won't be able to save her this time. I've already told you what's going to happen."

"She cares a lot about what happens to you. You do know that, don't you?"

Trent shook his head, keeping his weapon pressed against her head. "I don't want to hurt anyone, but I'm not going to spend the rest of my life in prison. All I need is a way out of here, and I'll disappear forever. Lexi won't get hurt, and the US government won't have to ever deal with me again."

Lexi stared at the ground a dozen feet in front of him. Lips tight, hands at her side. It was another no-win situation. But there had to be a way out of this where she didn't get hurt.

"The problem is, they're not going to agree to let you go," Colton said. "It's over, Trent. You've got to see that. There's no way you can make it to the border without getting caught. And if you kill Lexi now, you'll still be caught, or maybe even dead."

"Trent, please." Lexi's voice broke. "Don't end things this way."

"She's right," Colton said. "And even you know that everything's going to change if someone gets hurt. Or even worse if they die."

"No. You don't understand." His hand holding the gun started to shake. "I have to get out of here."

Colton took another a step forward. "You know that surrendering is the only way out of this alive."

Trent stared past him for a long while, then dropped the weapon onto the ground and put his hands up.

It was finally over.

Colton hurried over to where Lexi stood, watching them handcuff her brother. Shock registered on her expression. He pulled her into his arms and let her sob against his shoulder.

"I really thought he was going to kill me."

"He can't do anything to you now, but you're hurt," he said, noticing the blood on her arm and a makeshift bandage. "What happened?"

"It's nothing. Just a flesh wound from back at the compound."

"You're sure?"

She nodded.

"It's over, Lexi. For all of us. None of them can hurt you anymore."

She was crying harder now. Deep sobs that shook her body. He pulled her closer, knowing how personal this had become.

"I'm so sorry."

She looked up at him. "Being abducted by a stranger is one thing, but he's my brother. Maybe we've never been as close as I wanted, but he's still family."

"He was scared, Lexi, and in way over his head. Don't forget that. Fear makes people do crazy things."

"Like…like making me want to kiss you?"

Her question took him by surprise. She looked up at him with wide eyes, her body still trembling. Maybe he was nothing more to her than someone who'd been in the right place at the right time, but that's not how he felt. When he left Morocco, he wanted to leave knowing there was a chance for a relationship between them.

"Kiss me?" He smiled down at her. "I don't think that's crazy at all."

Colton forgot about everything going on around them as he pulled her tighter to him, then pressed his lips against hers.

Six hours later, Lexi stood in the corner of the US Embassy looking out over the manicured grounds. If she didn't know better, she'd think she was back in Washington, not Morocco. After finding her some clean clothes and letting her shower, one of the staff members had offered her something to eat. She'd declined as she knew she wouldn't be able hold anything down. Not yet. She still felt numb, and all her body really wanted to do was sleep.

But it was finally over.

The US ambassador had met with the three of them when they'd first arrived and had given them a brief update. Adam had been arrested along with Karim and five of his other men. There was no word yet on Salif, but according to the Malian government, they had already made at least a dozen arrests and were now closing in on the leader.

Which meant no more running. No more looking over her shoulder in fear.

But if that were true, then why did every shadow look like a ghost? Every person who came near her a possible assailant? She turned around as someone stepped into the room and felt the muscles in her shoulders tense.

"It's just me."

Colton walked past the long table in the center of the room over to where she was standing before offering her a cold drink.

"Thanks."

"I know you didn't eat. I could get you something."

"I'm okay for now." She popped open the top then took a long sip, hoping the caffeine didn't make her even more agitated. "I'm still feeling on edge. I can't stop thinking about Trent and what they're going to do with him."

And there was something else she couldn't stop thinking about. How she'd practically thrown herself at Colton.

"And I owe you an apology," she said.

"An apology? For what?"

"For asking you to kiss me."

Colton smiled, seemingly unruffled by the conversation. "If an apology is due, then I suppose I'm to blame, as well. I didn't exactly object."

"I know. It's just that... I wasn't... I'm not thinking straight."

Which was true. She'd been overwhelmed by the situation with Trent and how she felt about Colton.

"It's okay." He leaned against the edge of the table. "Everything you're feeling right now is normal. You know that, right? The lack of appetite...fatigue...edginess..."

"I know. I just can't seem to convince myself that we're not running anymore."

"There are a lot of reminders," he said, glancing at her arm where the bullet had grazed her. "What did the doctor say?"

She automatically reached for the spot the doctor had cleaned and bandaged. "It's just a flesh wound, though he started me on a round of antibiotics just to make sure there's no infection. It could have been so much worse."

"I agree. I keep telling myself how much we have to be thankful for. The three of us are alive and relatively unscathed. And they have the bad guys—or at least most of them—in custody."

"What about your sister?" Lexi asked, taking another long sip of the cold drink. "Have you been able to speak with her?"

"Bret's on the phone with her right now."

"How is she?"

"I left to give them some privacy, but I think she's

going to be okay. The FBI has determined that there's no longer a threat toward her, so she's gone home and has both her parents and in-laws with her for the time being."

"I bet Bret is ecstatic knowing he'll see them soon."

Colton's smile broadened. "Another thirty hours and he'll finally be home. It's been a long, hard journey for him. One I wasn't sure, to be honest, was actually going to happen."

"You risked your life for him, knowing this could have had a far different ending."

It was ironic, really. Colton had risked his life to save his brother-in-law, while her stepbrother's decisions had put her own life at risk. And ended his own freedom. But her feelings about her brother's betrayal were something she was going to have to explore another time when she had the emotional energy to deal with the situation. Right now, she just wanted to find a way to convince herself that Adam and Salif could no longer get to her.

She took another sip of her drink, then caught Colton's gaze studying hers. Her stomach flipped at their intensity and she looked away. Because she was trying to convince herself of more than the fact that she was no longer in danger. She couldn't deny she had feelings for him any more than she could deny the sense of safety he gave her when he was with her.

Because he was the kind of man she wanted to spend the rest of her life with. Honorable. Heroic. Funny.

Already their experience in the Sahara was beginning to feel like someone else's life. Something that she was ready to walk away from.

But was she ready to walk away from Colton, as well?

Her gaze settled on his lips for a brief moment. She knew the answer before she even asked the question. Despite the attraction she felt toward him—an attraction that had managed to transform into an undeniable connection—she could only see one way forward. Their lives were too different. Her heart was going to have to find a way to let go.

"What about your brother?" he asked, breaking into her thoughts.

She pressed her lips together. "He'll be flown back to the US to stand trial. I spoke briefly to my stepfather. He's struggling with the news. I know he's always prayed that Trent would start making the kind of decisions that would turn his life back around, but now…"

Now he was facing a steep prison sentence.

"And you?" Colton tossed his empty drink container into a metal trash can sitting in the corner of the room. "How are you dealing with the news?"

"I'm not even sure how I feel at this point. Mainly, I think I just feel sorry for him. He made choices that will affect the rest of his life. And that is going to be hard for us as his family to accept. And yet I still care about what happens to him." Lexi glanced out the window onto the manicured lawn and driveway, where there was a sudden flurry of activity. "What's going on down there?"

Colton hesitated before answering. "I was just speaking to the lieutenant who coordinated our rescue before I came in here. Most of the men who work for Adam will be tried here in this country, but they're preparing to take Adam to the US."

The thought of Adam being in the same building

as she was sent a new wave of panic through her. She looked outside the window where they stood. She saw him now. They were escorting him across the paved driveway toward a white van. The smirk he'd had when they were at his house had vanished, and in its place was anger.

"Lexi..."

She felt Colton's hand brush against her arm for support, but all she could see was Adam. He was walking, handcuffed, between three agents, staring at the brick paving. But instead of fear, a surprise wave of relief settled inside her. She'd been wrong. Seeing him again didn't bring with it the terror she'd expected. Instead, it brought a deepening sense of relief. Because she was free, and he was the one who was going to be spending the rest of his life in prison.

"Lexi?" Colton's fingers pressed around her elbow.

"I'm okay." She looked up and caught the concern in his eyes. "Really okay, actually. I didn't expect to feel this way, but there's a sense of closure in seeing him this way. A tangible reminder that this is really over."

"I agree. Listen...there's this great restaurant not far from here I'd like to try out. I was wondering if you were up to going there with me."

"I'm sorry, but I can't." A wave of disappointment swept over her, but she shook it off. This was how it had to be. And there was no use dragging out something that wasn't going to happen. "My teammates arranged for a bag of mine to be flown in from Timbuktu with my clothes, some personal things and my passport. As soon as it arrives later this evening, I'll be flying out. I'm actually headed to the airport in just a few minutes."

"Wow…that's great. For you."

"It is. I'm actually going to make it to Micah's wedding a couple days early."

A shadow crossed his face, causing her to pause.

"Here's the thing," he said. "I'd like to see you again, Lexi. I'd like to see if there's a chance for something to happen between us. I know that the last few days have been intense, but you're the kind of woman I've been looking for. Actually, I haven't really been looking, but the kind of woman I'd like to take a chance on getting to know."

Lexi forced herself to ignore the battle going on inside her. "I won't try and deny the fact that I do feel something, but, Colton, we live two very different lives and most of the time not even in the same country. And if I don't come back, we won't be living on the same continent."

"There are ways to make things work." He shot her a wide grin. "I'm a pilot, remember. I can always come see you."

She laughed, but her smile quickly faded. There was no way she was going to try another long-distance relationship. Best efforts and promises didn't work. And she didn't want another broken heart.

"I am grateful for everything," she said. "And maybe we'll run into each other again one day."

Though she knew the chances of that were slim. Which was why she needed to leave now and put everything about these past few days behind her.

She reached up and kissed him on the cheek, ignoring the pounding of her pulse at his nearness. "Goodbye, Colton."

But as she walked out the door, she couldn't help but wonder if it was already too late to avoid a broken heart.

EIGHTEEN

The restored castle in eastern Ireland with its lush green lawns couldn't be further from the hot desert sands of the Sahara. Lexi looked out of the window from the lavish bedroom with its Italian furniture and deep red walls to the stunning view of the lake surrounded by green lawns. It was yet another tangible reminder that she was finally safe.

Though safety was relative. While she'd been able to sleep fairly well since leaving Morocco, when she did dream, her dreams had been filled with frightening images of men with weapons chasing her through the desert.

Micah stood in front of a full-length mirror and adjusted the veil she was trying on with her jeans and a T-shirt. "I still can't believe you just said goodbye, then got on that plane."

Lexi sighed. "I barely know him."

It wasn't the first time they'd had this conversation. And knowing Micah, it wouldn't be the last. With only two days until her wedding, Micah had somehow become convinced that it was also her job to ensure everyone around her was living in the same blissful romantic fairy tale she was.

Yet as stunning as the setting was, Lexi's mind seemed unable to stop replaying the events of the past week. And if she were honest, yes, she was also finding it impossible to forget Colton.

Micah carefully pulled off the veil and set it back on the four-poster bed. "You might have only spent a few days with him, but from everything you've told me about what you went through, you had time to get to know him better than most people get to know someone over a matter of weeks...maybe months."

Lexi picked up the veil off the bed and put it neatly back in the hanging bag it had come in.

"If you don't care about him, then why do you look so glum?" Micah asked.

"I don't look glum."

"You do, and you need to call him. You need to see him again."

Lexi sighed. She should have remembered how stubborn Micah could be when she got her mind wrapped around something. But nothing she said was going to make a difference. Colton might have managed to wrap his way around her heart, but that didn't mean she shouldn't let him go. Everything she'd said had been true. Their lives were headed in different directions. They lived too far apart. And she had no intentions of taking a risk.

"You don't see it, do you?" Micah asked.

Lexi glanced up at Micah "See what?"

"You've been moody and distracted ever since you arrived."

She shook her head. "Did you ever stop to consider

that maybe it's because I went through a traumatic experience? Not because of a man?"

"Maybe it's both."

Lexi sat down on the edge of the bed. "Listen, I know you want me to find someone like you. And while I'm thrilled you're happy, I'm okay. Really. What Colton and I went through together did bond us together in a unique way, but that doesn't mean I'm ready to jump into a relationship with him."

"Why not? From everything I've heard about him—from you—he's perfect."

"I never said he was perfect, and besides…I thought Evan was perfect and look how that turned out."

Micah sat down beside her. "So that's what this is about. Evan."

Great. Here they went again. "Of course not."

"Look. Maybe Colton's the guy for you—maybe he isn't. But if you run way you're never going to know if he could have been the one. I just think you should give this guy a chance. Because if he is the one, trust me, it will be worth it."

Lexi frowned. She wasn't running away from anything. She was just being practical. And even more importantly, she was guarding her heart.

Colton grabbed the trash bag from under the kitchen sink in Bret and Becca's house, then secured the top. He was irritated. Distracted. And he was certain he knew the reason why. Forgetting Lexi had become impossible. He thought about her while he was awake, and she visited his dreams at night. Because the problem was she'd managed to steal his heart, then leave.

"Doctor just gave me a clean bill of health," Bret

said, walking into the kitchen with a huge smile on his face.

Colton dropped the trash and gave his brother-in-law a big hug. They'd been worried about a few possible side effects from his time in captivity. Hearing this was a huge answer to his prayer.

"So what are your plans for now?" Colton asked, quickly setting the trash in the bin just inside the garage.

"To get back to work as soon as I can."

"I was thinking more like a Caribbean cruise with your family," Colton said, shutting the door.

"Don't worry. Becca's already brought that up. And maybe we will. For the moment, being home with my family is enough for me."

"As long as you go easy on yourself. You've been through quite a lot."

Colton's phone rang and he pulled it out of his back pocket. No number came up for the caller ID, but he excused himself to step into the living room and answered it anyway.

"Hello?"

"Colton? This is Micah Young, Lexi's best friend. I'm here with her in Ireland right now."

"Micah...of course. She mentioned you." Colton hesitated. "Is she all right?"

"Physically, yes, but there's this heart issue I can't get her to admit to."

A heart issue?

"I don't understand," he said. "You mean some kind of medical issue?"

"Can I be perfectly frank?"

"Of course."

"Do you have feelings for her?"

Colton sat down on a leather recliner. That was not the question he'd been expecting.

"Yes, but I don't think that really matters," he said. "She made it pretty clear she wasn't interested in pursuing any kind of relationship."

"Maybe you already know this, but Lexi can be a bit…stubborn. And she'd kill me if she knew I was talking to you, but I'm positive she feels the same way you do."

His heart raced at the admission. Suddenly he was there with her again, in his mind, kissing her in the middle of the Sahara. "Okay so…did you have something in mind?"

"I do, actually. How soon can you get on a plane?"

"I'm sorry. A plane?"

"Think you could get on a flight to Ireland and be here in the next thirty-six hours and make it in time for my wedding?"

"And you wouldn't mind my showing up?" Colton asked.

"I called you, didn't I? You're like a real knight in shining armor. You swooped in and saved Lexi. I want you to come, but I also want you to surprise her."

Colton frowned. Somehow he'd assumed Lexi had been in on at least part of this. Like the part about him showing up at the wedding.

"Wait a minute. So she doesn't know about any of this? The phone call…your invitation to your wedding—"

"No."

Colton stared at the hardwood floor and shook his head. "Then we have a problem, because like I said, the last time I saw Lexi she was leaving and made it quite clear she wasn't interested in pursuing a relationship."

"I'm in the process of convincing her otherwise."

"You can't convince her to feel differently."

"Oh, I'm not. And trust me. You should see her. She's moody and down and spends half of her time staring out the window. This is all your fault, which means I need you to fix the situation."

His fault? Even if it was true, he could already think of a dozen things going wrong at his showing up. But he also knew how much he wanted to see Lexi again.

"Are you still there?" Micah asked.

"Yes, I'm just not sure your plan is going to work."

"Listen, I've known Lexi since we were in college. I've heard her talk about you, and I know she's crazy about you. She's just afraid to admit that she's already lost her heart. But she has. Trust me."

Colton rubbed the back of his neck, still not completely convinced. He'd already sent Lexi an email. Just a brief note, checking on how she was doing. Her response had been short. She was doing well. Busy preparing for the wedding. No emotion. No hint that she had any desire to see him again. Clearly anything that he'd thought had passed between them had been only in his head and nothing more. Wasn't it?

If he walked away now, he'd never know for sure.

"Okay. I'll be there." The words were out before he had time to fully process what he was agreeing to.

"Perfect. You find something to wear, and I'll have someone pick you up at the airport and make sure you have a place to stay with the wedding party."

"You don't have to do all of this."

"Lexi's my best friend. She deserves to be as happy

as I do. And something tells me that despite all the horrible things that happened to the two of you, this is going to be another happy-ever-after ending after all."

Lexi adjusted Micah's veil for the final time, then checked her watch. There was still forty-five minutes until the wedding was to start and everything on Lexi's list was finally checked off.

She smiled at her best friend. The veil was perfect. The dress was perfect. Even the weather had cooperated and was perfect.

"You look beautiful," she said.

Micah's smile widened. "Thank you. I can't believe my wedding day is finally here."

This could be me and Colton one day.

The thought surfaced unexpectedly. Lexi's gaze shifted back to the intricate beading on Micah's dress. How many times as a little girl had she imagined herself in a beautiful white wedding dress marrying her own knight in shining armor?

What if she'd found that knight and let him go?

Lexi pressed her lips together as she grabbed Micah's white ballet slippers out of their box and started helping her slip them on. Lexi had a legitimate reason for walking away. She had to protect her heart from getting hurt again.

Except Colton was nothing like Evan.

Their experience together in North Africa had proved that to her, and showed her that he was the kind of man she wanted to spend the rest of her life with. No, *the* man she wanted to spend the rest of her life with.

And yet she'd pushed Colton away, and now...what

if it was too late? Because no matter how hard she tried to fight it, she loved him.

"Lexi, what's wrong?" Micah asked, putting on the second shoe.

She tossed the box back on the bed. "Nothing."

"I know you better than that. What's going on?"

Lexi blinked back the tears, wishing she could stomp down all the *what if* questions that kept popping up. She was being emotional. She knew no one would blame her after everything she'd just been through, but today was Micah's day. Not hers.

"Really, it's nothing." She stood up and forced a smile. "Seeing you as a bride and knowing you're about to get married must be rubbing off on me. That whole romantic notion of falling in love and living happily ever after."

Micah rested her hands against her hips. "It's Colton, isn't it?"

"Of course not." She shook her head, but knew she couldn't avoid the truth. Not with Micah. "Okay. Maybe. It's just that I can't help but wonder if I made a mistake? I told him goodbye and walked away, but what if I was wrong." She drew in a sharp breath. "What if I love him?"

Micah's smile was back. "If you love him, then I think you should tell him."

A knock on the door of the changing room, interrupted their conversation.

"Miss Shannon?"

Lexi opened the door. "Yes."

"There's someone on the balcony downstairs who would like to see you. They said it's urgent."

"Are you sure they want me?" she asked.

"If you're Lexi Shannon, then yes."

Who in the world would be here to see her?

"Just hurry down there, will you?" Micah said. "I'll go find my bouquet."

"It was in my room the last time I saw it. I could go now—"

"No. I'll get it. Go."

Lexi frowned, then hurried into the hallway. She could see the green lawns from the windows as she made her way downstairs. Such a contrast from the harsh terrain and dull colors of the desert. The crazy thing was that she still felt this strange urge to return despite everything she'd experienced. Because as well as the evils she'd seen, she'd seen the beauty of both the landscape and the people. And it was something she could never forget.

She just needed time. Time to figure out what she wanted to do next. Go back to Africa or find somewhere else to use her skills. And more importantly, figure out what to do about the man who'd managed to steal her heart.

Lexi stepped out onto the balcony, then froze. He was standing with the sun on his back. The same sandy-haired pilot she'd met all those months ago. Black suit with a white shirt and a thin black tie. Perfect for a wedding. Her heart pounded and she couldn't breathe.

"Colton."

He shot her a smile. "Hey. Wow. You look stunning."

She glanced down at the purple dress. For a bridesmaid dress, Micah had chosen well. But she couldn't think about that. Not now.

"What are you doing here?" she asked.

"I was invited to a wedding."

Micah.

"I... I don't know what to say. I just... They told me someone wanted to see me, but I never thought..." She was babbling. But her racing pulse and pounding heart, confirmed everything she'd just said to Micah.

She loved him.

He took a step forward, still smiling at her. "You could start with 'Thanks for the compliment, and it's great to see you.' At least I hope it is."

She smiled back, certain this was some crazy dream. There was no way Colton was actually here standing in front of her. He was supposed to have gone to see his family. How was he here beside her in a five-hundred-year-old castle in Ireland?

"It is great to see you," she said, breathing in the spicy scent of his cologne while trying to convince herself he was really here. "I just didn't expect it."

"The surprise part was Micah's idea. I hope she was right. She was pretty convincing."

"She's always been stubborn. And a romantic."

"Here's the thing." He moved closer and ran his fingers across her arm sending shivers down her spine. "I haven't been able to stop thinking about you. About us. I know you said you weren't interested in a long-distance relationship, but I'm not ready to just walk away. I believe we can make this work. Because the bottom line is, Lexi, I'm in love with you."

Her mind spun. Five minutes ago she'd wondered if she'd made the biggest mistake of her life walking away from him, and now Colton was standing in front of her telling her he loved her.

"I was talking to the director of our team," he continued before she could respond. "They're looking for someone to head up a new station. It's a bit remote, though of course with a plane you're never that far from civilization. In another six months they're hoping to add a water project. There's a huge need for clean water in this area. You'd be done with your assignment in Timbuktu, and if you felt like sticking around, I know for a fact they'd welcome you on board."

"Colton, wait—"

"I'm sorry." He shook his head. "This is all too fast, isn't it? I told Micah I couldn't just show up and convince you to feel something you didn't feel."

"No." She reached out to straighten his tie, then let her hands linger on his chest, still feeling breathless. "I was going to say you don't have to convince me of anything, Colton."

"I don't?"

"No, you don't."

She might have gotten hurt when Evan walked out on her, but her heart knew that this was different. That Colton was different. He'd proved he was willing to risk his own life for the lives of those he cared about. Risk his life for people he didn't even know. He was loyal and trustworthy.

And she had been foolish to believe she could simply walk away and forget him. Because she did love him, and he was the one she wanted to be with the rest of her life.

"I know I'm not making sense, but I'm still trying to take in the fact that you're standing in front of me. And in a suit and tie no less,."

She drew in a deep breath. "The truth is I haven't been able to stop thinking about you either. I tried to convince myself that what I feel toward you is nothing more than what any girl would feel about the handsome hero who swooped in and rescued her, but that isn't true. I want this to work between us."

"For a lifetime, maybe?" He took her hands and pulled her closer against him. Her heart felt as if it had stopped beating.

"Yeah…a lifetime."

She wrapped her arms around his neck. "I think this is the part when you're supposed to kiss me again."

He smiled down at her. "I don't know. I hear fear is what makes people do crazy things. Like kissing."

Her breath caught as he brushed his lips against hers. "It looks to me that while *Casablanca* might not have had a perfect happily-ever-after ending, I'm going to get mine."

* * * * *

If you enjoyed this exciting internationally set
suspense story, pick up these other titles
by Lisa Harris:

FINAL DEPOSIT
STOLEN IDENTITY
DEADLY SAFARI
TAKEN
DESPERATE ESCAPE

Available now from Love Inspired Suspense!

Find more great reads at www.LoveInspired.com.

Dear Reader,

I've had people ask me if I've experienced some of the things I put my characters through, and thankfully I could always say no. While a lot of people love an adrenaline rush, I don't, and I certainly have no desire to experience any of the scenarios from my suspense novels. But while I was in the process of finishing this story, three armed men walked into our house, tied up my family and robbed us.

The experience changed how I felt about a lot of things, including writing suspense. Before I could continue, I had to rethink why I write what I write. I was eventually able to move forward and pour my emotions from the attack into this story, which ended up bringing me healing. And I hope that once you've read this story, you'll remember the fact that the God who created the universe wants to be your refuge and fortress— no matter what you are going through.

Be blessed,
Lisa Harris

COMING NEXT MONTH FROM
Love Inspired® Suspense

Available March 7, 2017

MISTAKEN IDENTITY
Mission: Rescue • by Shirlee McCoy

When Trinity Miller's attacked by a man who believes she's Mason Gains's girlfriend, the former army pilot turned reclusive prosthetic maker is forced from seclusion to rescue her. But the assailant won't stop targeting her—unless Mason gives up information on one of his clients.

HER BABY'S PROTECTOR
by Margaret Daley and Susan Sleeman

As babies are thrust into danger in two brand-new novellas, these men will stop at nothing to keep them—and their lovely single mothers—safe.

PLAIN SANCTUARY • by Alison Stone
Running her new Amish community bed-and-breakfast, Heather Miller believes she's finally safe from her violent ex-husband—until he escapes from prison to come after her. Now her only hope of survival is relying on US Marshal Zach Walker for protection.

THE SEAL'S SECRET CHILD
Navy SEAL Defenders • by Elisabeth Rees

When former SEAL Edward "Blade" Harding receives an email from his six-year-old son, he's shocked—both by the news that he has a child and by his son's message. Someone's threatening to kill Blade's ex-fiancée, defense attorney Josie Bishop…and she and their little boy need his help.

SECURITY DETAIL
Secret Service Agents • by Lisa Phillips

A mobster is after the former president's daughter Kayla Harris, and she's not sure why. But undercover Secret Service agent Conner Thorne's determined to find out…and save her life.

OUTSIDE THE LAW • by Michelle Karl
Former military recruit Yasmine Browder plans to uncover the truth about her brother's death…but her investigation quickly turns deadly. And her childhood friend rookie FBI agent Noel Black risks his career—and his life—to help her solve the mystery.

REQUEST YOUR FREE BOOKS!

2 FREE RIVETING INSPIRATIONAL NOVELS
PLUS 2 FREE MYSTERY GIFTS

SUSPENSE

RIVETING INSPIRATIONAL ROMANCE

YES! Please send me 2 FREE Love Inspired® Suspense novels and my 2 FREE mystery gifts (gifts are worth about $10). After receiving them, if I don't wish to receive any more books, I can return the shipping statement marked "cancel." If I don't cancel, I will receive 4 brand-new novels every month and be billed just $4.99 per book in the U.S. or $5.49 per book in Canada. That's a savings of at least 17% off the cover price. It's quite a bargain! Shipping and handling is just 50¢ per book in the U.S. and 75¢ per book in Canada.* I understand that accepting the 2 free books and gifts places me under no obligation to buy anything. I can always return a shipment and cancel at any time. Even if I never buy another book, the two free books and gifts are mine to keep forever.

123/323 IDN GH5Z

Name _____ (PLEASE PRINT) _____

Address _____ Apt. # _____

City _____ State/Prov. _____ Zip/Postal Code _____

Signature (if under 18, a parent or guardian must sign)

Mail to the **Reader Service:**
IN U.S.A.: P.O. Box 1867, Buffalo, NY 14240-1867
IN CANADA: P.O. Box 609, Fort Erie, Ontario L2A 5X3

**Are you a current subscriber to Love Inspired® Suspense books
and want to receive the larger-print edition?
Call 1-800-873-8635 or visit www.ReaderService.com.**

* Terms and prices subject to change without notice. Prices do not include applicable taxes. Sales tax applicable in N.Y. Canadian residents will be charged applicable taxes. Offer not valid in Quebec. This offer is limited to one order per household. Not valid for current subscribers to Love Inspired Suspense books. All orders subject to credit approval. Credit or debit balances in a customer's account(s) may be offset by any other outstanding balance owed by or to the customer. Please allow 4 to 6 weeks for delivery. Offer available while quantities last.

Your Privacy—The Reader Service is committed to protecting your privacy. Our Privacy Policy is available online at www.ReaderService.com or upon request from the Reader Service.
We make a portion of our mailing list available to reputable third parties that offer products we believe may interest you. If you prefer that we not exchange your name with third parties, or if you wish to clarify or modify your communication preferences, please visit us at www.ReaderService.com/consumerschoice or write to us at Reader Service Preference Service, P.O. Box 9062, Buffalo, NY 14240-9062. Include your complete name and address.